Something Old, Something New
by Maggie Casper

Traveling west from Boston is the adventure of a lifetime for mail order bride, Matilda Cummings—until she learns her soon-to-be husband, Dawson Chandler, had no use for a wife.

Switching places with her twin sister to become a mail order bride seemed like the thing to do, until feisty Matilda Cummings reaches the wilds of Dodge City and finds out her soon-to-be husband hadn't seen fit to meet her train, sending his brother instead.

Dawson Chandler wants more than anything to strangle his younger brother when he learns he's unwittingly signed a binding marriage contract. He's got no use for a wife, especially the tiny, prissy looking woman whose picture haunts him. A lady, polished and shined, has no business living on the Rocking C Ranch, nor with a man like himself.

Afraid of hurting a delicate woman with his rough and tumble ways, Dawson never plans to marry. After all, why should he shackle himself to a lady when he prefers the experience of a seasoned whore in the bedroom? Much to his dismay, he finds his little lady is nothing like he'd imagines. Soon, Dawson and Matilda find themselves struggling through not only their physical but emotional relationships in search of love. Will they find it?

Something Borrowed, Something Blue
by Lena Matthews

Wedding consultant Azure Kerr has seen the best of what love has to offer...professionally. Personally, she's been too busy to find a love of her own. That all changes the day sexy stranger Gavin Conner comes knocking at her door.

But love, for Gavin, is a matter of once burnt, twice shy. When Azure finds a storied plum-colored wedding gown—and decides she wants to wear it—can Gavin overcome his fears and persuade her to wear it for him?

A Sixpence in Her Shoe
by Liz Andrews

Can Melanie Parsons trust Brady Torres with her most trusted possession—her heart?
Melanie Parsons is a curator at the Smithsonian, specializing in nineteenth and twentieth century artifacts. A rash of burglaries causes Brady Torres, a member of United Americas Security, to be called in to investigate.

Melanie comes from a Traditionalist family, a fundamental group of individuals who want to return to the ideals of an earlier time. Although she doesn't believe in those ideals, especially when it comes to marriage, she has two little secrets. She loves for a man to control her in the bedroom and the particular man she is longing to take that control is none other than Agent Brady Torres.

The UAS believes Traditionalists are behind the burglaries, but Brady is not sold on the idea and proposes they use a wedding dress from the 1800s as bait to capture the thieves. The dress, from Melanie's own family, is the one thing that keeps Brady believing he might have a chance with Melanie. He figures she wouldn't keep the dress around if she didn't secretly harbor a desire to find true love and marry for a lifetime.

If Brady loses the dress to the thieves will he also lose his chance with Melanie?

Warning, this title contains the following: explicit sex, graphic language, light bondage

The Wedding Dress

Maggie Casper
Lena Matthews
&
Liz Andrews

A Samhain Publishing, Ltd. publication.

Samhain Publishing, Ltd.
2932 Ross Clark Circle, #384
Dothan, AL 36301
www.samhainpublishing.com

The Wedding Dress
ISBN: 1-59998-281-1

Editing by Jessica Bimberg, Teri Smith
Cover by Anne Cain

Something Old, Something New electryonic publication: August 2006
Something Borrowed, Something Blue: electronic publication: August 2006
A Sixpence In Her Shoe: electronic publication: August 2006

Contents

Something Old, Something New

Maggie Casper

Dedication

To Lena Matthews and Liz Andrews for including me when the idea for the Wedding Dress series hit.

Chapter One

Matilda Cummings had never been so glad to see the caboose of a train as she was when she finally reached Dodge City. Her skirts were littered with burns from the engine's relentless spewing of sparks and her hair was misbehaving something fierce. All in all, she knew she must look a fright. Wearing numerous layers of clothing and the need to act prim and proper all the time was taxing on one's body.

Not for the first time since leaving her home in Boston did Matilda curse her twin sister, Melinda, for getting her into this mess. And yet, if she was completely honest with herself, she would admit she'd jumped at the idea of such a grand adventure.

Of course, this was before she'd spent days cramped into the hot interior of a train car with too many unwashed bodies to count. Matilda wrinkled her nose at the memory as she soaked her tired and achy bones in the luxury of a hot bath.

After stepping from the train, Matilda hadn't been sure she'd actually be able to find the respectable hotel where her soon-to-be-husband had made arrangements. And wandering around alone was completely out of the question. She'd been warned before leaving home of the lawless behavior found in Dodge City but even her wildest imaginings hadn't done the place justice.

She remained on the North side of the railroad tracks just as she'd been instructed to, and once she'd found a trusting soul to ask directions, she'd hired a hackney to take her to her lodgings for the night.

Mr. Chandler, her husband-to-be, had warned it might be late in the day before he made it into the city. Evidently, the Rocking C Ranch was nearly fifty miles from Dodge City, a trip Matilda was not looking forward to, but would make without complaint, nonetheless.

After the tedious task of drying her hair and dressing, Matilda was famished. She warily made her way down the staircase and through the lobby to the connecting dining room, happy she wouldn't actually have to leave the building.

As she entered the dining room, Matilda was pleased to see just how well kept the place was. Like her room, it was as neat as a pin. Checked tablecloths covered the tabletops and the floor was shined to a high gloss. Clean and starched curtains hung in the windows, their pristine white nearly blinding in intensity.

Matilda tried not to notice how several people, men and women alike, stared at her as she entered the dining room. Long ago she'd learned not to be offended by sly gazes and outright stares to her overly large bosom. Matilda patted her hair and smoothed her skirts instead of scowling as she really wished to do. Didn't they know it was impolite to stare?

"Right this way, miss." A man with a nasally voice led her to a table.

Matilda was just preparing to sit when a man—a very tall, very handsome in a clean cut sort of way man—stopped beside her table. "Excuse me, ma'am but might you be Miss Cummings, Miss M. Cummings of Boston?"

The way her heart fluttered against her breast made her feel a bit lightheaded. If the man in front of her was to be her husband, Matilda figured she'd either be in heaven always or in hell for an eternity for all the wayward thoughts rolling through her mind.

It took her a minute to realize she was standing there, staring like some addle-brained child barely out of the schoolroom.

"Yes. Yes, I am. And you are?"

A flush stole up the gentleman's neck to rest on his cheeks. His piercing green gaze darted away for a second before coming back to rest on her. He thrust his hand out and introduced himself. "I'm Duncan. Duncan Chandler, Dawson's younger brother."

Matilda had numerous questions she wanted answered, the first being why hadn't her soon to be husband seen fit to pick her up instead of sending his brother, but etiquette required she shake hands and be polite before interrogating the man.

"Mr. Chandler." Matilda murmured her greeting at the same time as she placed her hand in his.

"Shall I set another place, miss?" the waiter inquired before seating the both of them and then hurrying off at her nod of approval.

"I hope your trip wasn't too taxing?"

He asked the question with sincerity. For a second, Matilda wanted to groan and grumble about the hellacious conditions she'd been exposed to on the long trip but she didn't. Complaining wasn't in her nature. She was more of a hold-it-all-in-until-you-explode kind of girl.

Matilda decided to get straight to the point. After all, she was the one who had traveled across country. She had a right to know what was going on since it concerned her directly.

"Where is the other Mr. Chandler, the one who is to be my husband, and why didn't he accompany you?"

Kind green eyes stared back at her. "Can I be frank with you?"

More than anything Matilda wanted to roll her eyes. Why did men just assume women wanted to be coddled and lied to?

"Yes, I do believe it would be for the best if you were."

It was getting harder and harder to play the part of the prim and proper miss her mother continually reminded her she was.

"My brother Dawson, the man who is as good as your husband, wasn't aware he'd signed a marriage contract. As a result of my meddling, not only is he not speaking to me but he refused to make the trip to meet your train much less accompany me on the same errand."

For the first time since she could remember, Matilda could find no words to convey the overwhelming amount of dismay burning a hole in her stomach. But she opened her mouth and made an effort anyway.

"Well, yes. I see. So I am to travel back to Boston then?" She wasn't going to strangle the man or shoot a hole in him with the small pearl-handled pistol she kept in her reticule and she surely wasn't going to cry although the tears burning the back of her throat boasted otherwise.

This time the fool-headed man actually smiled. "The only traveling you'll be doing is with me and my men to the Rocking C."

"I'm afraid I don't understand, Mr. Chandler."

"Duncan."

Matilda couldn't help but stare at his clean-shaven face, a face which a mere minute ago had seemed kind and yet now bore a glint of stubbornness. Choosing to pick her battles wisely, Matilda nodded. "Duncan. I'm afraid I do not understand. If the other Mr. Chandler does not wish me for his wife, why would I continue on my journey to your ranch?"

A wicked grin curved his lips and Matilda bet every woman within a twenty-mile radius had, at one time or another, been affected by his charm. His next words, though, set her back on her chair and reminded her once again to never place trust in those you didn't know well.

"I may have been meddling but I still believe I did what was best for Dawson. He signed the contract, willing or not, and you are here so things will go on as intended."

Stubborn or not, Matilda was not going to be chained to a man who wanted nothing to do with her. Scooting her chair away from the table, she made to rise. "Well then I will be the reasonable one and call it off. If your brother wants no part of a wife then I'll not force him to it."

It was hard to admit just how much it hurt to know the man thought so little of her he couldn't even pull himself away long enough to meet her train and see to her welfare.

A hand on her sleeve stopped her. "Please sit, Miss Cummings."

For a moment, Matilda thought about refusing. She gave a quick glance around the room and knew to do so would make quite a scene. Since the stubborn angle of Duncan's jaw gave the impression he could care less what others thought, she did as he asked.

"Thank you." He inclined his head when she resumed her seat.

Leaning forward, Matilda whispered furiously. "I do not understand why you are so set on this, Mr. Chandler, but I do not intend to become chattel for a man who does not require a wife."

"It's Duncan. Don't forget it again and as for the rest, the contract has been signed and is binding. You are already as good as married. Unless..." He let his words trail off, keeping Matilda in suspense.

"What is it Mr....Duncan?"

"Unless you have the stage fare to return?"

Matilda had some money hidden in the hem of her petticoats as well as a bit in her reticule but not nearly enough to pay back what she would owe if she were to back out of the contract.

"I see from the expression on your face you do not." This time it was Duncan who stood. "I'll call for you first thing in the morning, Miss Cummings. Please wear something comfortable as it will take several days of traveling to reach the Rocking C."

The big oaf turned, dismissing her as if her word on the matter counted for nothing.

"I will not." Oh God, please spare her highhanded men, she thought several seconds later when he turned back around to face her.

With his palms flat on the table, nearly nose to nose, Duncan growled. "If you are not ready first thing tomorrow morning, I will have to bring you in front of the judge for going against a binding contract."

"You wouldn't!" It was outrageous to even think it.

"Try me, sweetheart."

The man was a barbarian. "You, sir, are no gentleman." Then Matilda had an idea. "I'll accompany you to the judge then."

For a moment, Duncan seemed as if he might possibly swallow his tongue. His face had grown red in anger and he seemed to be shocked at her willfulness.

"And pray tell what is it you would say to the man?"

Matilda swallowed past the lump in her throat. Her bluff was not going to work, she could already tell. "I will explain the whole ordeal. I will tell him how you bamboozled your brother into signing a contract. The contract is void, Mr. Chandler, because your brother was unaware of what he was signing. I am sure the judge will see it that way as well."

Duncan once again took the seat across from her. His smile grew even more feral and gone was the kind man who had first approached her. In his place was a ruthless rancher dressed as a gentleman.

"You think so do you? I think he will see Dawson's signature and not care how it got there. The one thing I am curious about is how he will feel about being duped by you, Miss Cummings."

"Duped? By Me?" Good grief! She sounded like an idiot.

"Yes, by you. You see, during our last correspondence you, or should I say your sister, cousin, aunt, you fill in the blank, Miss Cummings, sent me a likeness of herself. You may very well be M. Cummings, but you are not the M. Cummings who promised herself in a contract of marriage."

Damn, damn, double damn, Matilda cursed silently in her head. Duncan held a small photo of her sister in his palm. As always, Melinda was dressed impeccably. Not a hair out of place on her skinny little head. She didn't boast the round cheeks or deep dimples Matilda herself did.

"Am I to assume we've come to an agreement then?"

She didn't want to admit the inevitable but was left no choice in the matter. Her goose was as good as cooked. "Yes."

"It'll be a long trip, Miss Cummings. I suggest we do it as friends rather than enemies. My only intention here was to find a wife for my brother, not ruin your life in the process. If it is any consolation, your fire and strength of character might actually be better than the meek and biddable wife I had originally planned for my brother. At the very least, it will keep me entertained."

Then, with another bright smile, Duncan nodded his farewell and left the dining room and Matilda, who was still trying to sort through all that had just taken place.

CB80

Much later the same night, Matilda lay staring at the water-stained ceiling of her room. She had pushed a chair beneath the handle of the door after locking it. After all, a woman alone couldn't be too careful.

She couldn't seem to get Duncan Chandler out of her mind. Her first thought was it was probably a good thing he wasn't to be her husband because they would more than likely end up killing or at the very least, seriously maiming each other.

The way he had waltzed into the dining room of her hotel with a kind smile curving his lips only to turn out to be the devil himself. Just thinking about their conversation made her irate.

On the other hand, he wasn't completely unlikable. He evidently had his older brother's best interest at heart. So although he was insufferably arrogant and too handsome for his own usefulness, he was to be her brother-in-law and so Matilda would do her best to forgive him his faults.

Dawson Chandler paced the length of the kitchen and back again. By his estimation, Duncan and Miss Cummings, the woman he was due to marry, should be lumbering up the road in the buckboard any time now.

After nearly two weeks, he'd begun to worry and, as a result, had sent a small group of men to scout for his long lost brother. Just this morning, one of the men had ridden into the ranch yard to announce he'd spotted a small caravan carrying not only Duncan and Miss Cummings, but a group of Rocking C men with enough supplies to last for months.

He couldn't get the vision of the photograph of a scrawny Miss Cummings out of his mind. She appeared breakable and delicate, a combination which scared Dawson to no end.

Her top had been buttoned clear up to her ears it seemed and her hair looked as though no one ever had or ever would run their fingers through it. She was probably the type who would insist on going to bed clothed from head to toe and only doing the deed in the dark of night.

Dawson shuddered at the thought. If she was going to end up his wife, there would be ground rules long before any ceremony took place.

He'd just come to his conclusion when the rumbling of wagon wheels vibrated the plank floor of the ranch house. Taking a deep breath and praying for patience, Dawson made his way out the kitchen door and moved toward the barn where Duncan was helping Miss Cummings down from the high seat of the buckboard.

From his vantage point, Dawson saw the scowl she sent Duncan's way before smoothing her skirts and reaching for the carpetbag he still held in his hands.

The first thing he noticed was how the long, dark tendrils of hair, which had escaped the pins she'd no doubt tried to control them with, seemed to have a life all their own. Completely bypassing her face, his gaze settled on the overly generous curve of her chest. Good Lord Almighty! Either the photo had done her a great injustice or she'd sprouted an abundance of curves since it had been commissioned.

Realizing he was just about to reach her, Dawson lifted his gaze to her face. What he saw there was enough to steal his breath. Round cheeks with twin dimples framed the most luscious bow of a mouth he had ever seen and before he could stop it, his cock responded by swelling to life.

"Mr. Chandler." She offered her hand and although tiny in comparison to his, her grip was firm.

"Miss Cummings, I presume?"

It had been years since the mere sight and slight touch of a woman, any woman, had stirred his desire so strongly. The thought turned Dawson's mood black. If the woman standing before him were like any other, she would take the power her body held and turn it against him. Women like her were one of the many reasons why Dawson preferred the company of a seasoned whore over a lady any night of the week.

The small smile curving her lips disappeared. "Y-yes."

Keeping his facial expression blank, he looked into the dark wells of her eyes without releasing his hold on her hand. Their depths were unfathomable and gave away everything she was feeling. Her unease was almost palpable and would probably grow to insurmountable limits before they had worked out all the details of their relationship.

Although not normally spoken of, Dawson planned to speak on every subject including the sexual aspect of their marriage and he planned to have it all spelled out for Miss Cummings long before a preacher pronounced them man and wife.

"Right this way then. I'll show you to your room so you can get settled. Tomorrow we'll talk." His cock twitched just thinking about her in the room adjoining his, but until things were worked out to his liking, her room was exactly where she was going to stay.

Chapter Two

Matilda's first thought, as she unpacked a few of her belongings, was how lovely the room was. She'd not had many expectations but the sheer size of the house was overwhelming. It stood strong and tall on a plateau. Its two stories rose above the ground to nearly the heights of a few of the surrounding oak trees.

The house fit the man for Dawson was a large man, larger than any Matilda had ever before laid eyes on. He'd been dressed in denims and a button-down shirt. The pants were snug and fit like a second skin, leaving her eyes wide and her heart pounding against her chest. It had been hard to pull her gaze away, instead concentrating on the interior of the house.

From the looks of it, the Chandler men were not too keen on decorating. No frilly curtains adorned the windows downstairs and no colorful rugs covered the floors.

The room she'd been supplied was just a bit different though. Her windows had the sheerest of covering in a light and airy peach color, setting off the floral spread tucked neatly into the edges of what appeared to be a very fluffy mattress. After spending many days and nights traveling and sleeping either in a seated position or on the ground beneath the stars, the thought of a mattress like on her bed at home nearly brought tears to her eyes.

Knowing Dawson's room adjoined hers kept Matilda a bit on edge. He gave no reason why he chose the room he did. He'd said nothing at all, which bothered Matilda to no end. She wasn't quite sure why. Could it be because after leaving her to unpack and rest he'd probably gone off and completely forgotten about her? After all, he didn't want a wife or companion. From the looks of him, he could have any woman he crooked his finger at. His single state was obviously planned. His bachelorhood held onto tightly just as a spinster held tightly to her unmentionables.

Well, Matilda had no intention of letting his meddling brother or him get to her. She'd packed up and moved West with the intention of experiencing a grand adventure and she planned to do just that, whether as a married woman or not.

Not one to sit idly by, much to her mother's chagrin, Matilda quickly stripped down to her chemise and corset in order to freshen up. Critically, she viewed herself in the small mirror hanging above the wash basin. The pink half moons of her nipples peeked over the top of her corset and showed clearly through the thin fabric of her chemise. She was by no means a small woman. In some places her curves had curves but she no longer bemoaned the fact as she had when still a young girl in pigtails.

Giving silent thanks to whoever had seen to the preparations of her room, Matilda poured water from the large mouth pitcher into the matching basin. Once finished, she then proceeded to lather up a soft cloth and wash her face and body.

Although not nearly as wonderful as a hot bath, the clean smelling soap and cool water were very refreshing. Now if she could just dispense with the corset squeezing her so tightly around the middle she half feared being cut in two.

"Not likely to happen." Her mumbled response sounded sulky even to her own ears. But oh how she hated wearing the contraption. She longed to don a pair of jeans and button-down shirt almost as much as she missed the feel of grass beneath her feet.

Her mother had lectured and warned before she'd left home on how improper it would be to get caught enjoying either. Matilda huffed, irritation riding her hard. Although tired, she was not the least bit sleepy. Instead of doing as Dawson suggested, she dressed in another blouse and long skirt.

The house was large and, with very little effort, could be stunningly beautiful. The overwhelming urge to explore set her on a path down the hallway. She quietly descended the stairs then made her way to the back of the house where she assumed the kitchen was located.

She wasn't the best of cooks, not having much time for practice, but she did have a powerfully passionate love for food so planned to learn all the Rocking C's cook was willing to teach her. Matilda heard the clanging of pots and pans before reaching the kitchen. With every intention of introducing herself, she entered the kitchen, nearly squinting at the stark whiteness of the walls. The place was shiny clean, so clean Matilda was afraid to touch anything.

"Oh!" The startled yelp was accompanied by the loud clatter of metal falling onto the wooden floorboards. "Dear Lord, you scared the pee outta me."

Matilda couldn't help but giggle at the woman's choice of words. She was very tall for a woman, towering over Matilda's petite frame. "I didn't mean to scare you, Miss…" Matilda asked, hinting at the woman's name.

"You call me Jess and we'll do just fine." Jess picked the pan she'd dropped up off the floor before turning her attention back to Matilda.

Matilda immediately liked Jess. She seemed very open and honest and not at all stuffy like those she was used to dealing with. "And I'm Matilda. Matilda Cummings."

"So glad you made it safe and sound, Miss Matilda. Duncan, the scoundrel, didn't bother to come in and greet me properly." Jess' lips curved in a smile before she continued, "He's probably hiding in the barn hoping to stay out of Dawson's long reach. Those two still fight like youngsters, I tell ya. Of course, that has a way of happening when your brother marries you off without your say so. Lordy, Lordy. I thought those two would tear each other up when Duncan finally admitted what he'd gone and done."

Then, as if finally realizing her faux pas, Jess clamped her mouth shut. "Good grief, listen to me go on and on." With her cheeks pink, she spun around and continued whatever it was she'd been doing before Matilda had interrupted her.

"Is there something I could help you do?"

Just as quickly as she'd spun away, Jess turned back to her. She gave Matilda one of the most beautiful smiles she'd ever seen. "If you've a mind to help this big ninny, then I'm all for it."

Matilda assumed Jess was referring to what she'd said earlier pertaining to Duncan and his meddling but decided not to ask any questions. "Well then, show me what needs doing."

For the next hour, Matilda and Jess worked side by side getting the evening meal on the table. At one point, while Matilda peeled potatoes, Dawson came in through the kitchen door. He seemed surprised to see her sitting at the table, hard at work. His surprise was short lived, a mask of indifference quickly taking its place.

"Since it seems you're not overly tired, we'll have our talk now." There was something in his eyes, something untamed. Where Duncan's eyes had been the piercing green of emerald, Dawson's were soft, like moss with flecks of gold throughout. His hair was long, nearly to his collar and deep russet in color. The way it fell in rakish waves over his brow made Matilda's fingers itch to feel its texture.

She wasn't even sure what to think of the stubble covering his jaw. Was he allowing a beard to grow out? Matilda was pulled from her silent perusal of him when, without waiting for her approval, Dawson took her hand in his and led her from the room. Dawson's hand upon hers was quite shocking to Matilda's system. Her flesh pebbled and tingled from head to toe with her more feminine spots nearly hurting from the intensity.

Oh, she might be pure, the way an unwed woman her age was supposed to be, but she was far from sheltered about the intimacies between a man and a woman. Her mother had been outrageously clear on what would happen once she was good and properly wed. Matilda's face still heated every time she thought of the conversation. It was amazing to think men and women actually did such things when shrouded by the darkness of night and the blankets upon their bed.

Dawson noticed the blush working its way up her face and wondered if it started at the overly generous swell of her breast. He mumbled a curse because once again, she'd sidetracked his train of thought. Not only that, but instead of working, he'd accomplished nothing this afternoon except for daydreams about burying his face in what was sure to be magnificently ample cleavage.

She was once again buttoned nearly to her chin with her skirt reaching the floor, not even a quick peek at bare ankle was to be had. Dawson walked blindly through the house trying his best not to inhale her womanly scent. His cock was hard and ready from the feel of her small hand held tightly within his.

When they finally made it to the study, Dawson heaved a silent sigh of relief. In this room he felt comfortable. It was still furnished the same as it had been when his father was alive. The same large mahogany desk with its carved foliage edging graced the farthest wall of the room, as did the same overstuffed chair behind it.

The scent of pipe smoke and leather book bindings welcomed Dawson every time he entered the room. The room, as well as the house, had made it through drought and famine, lawlessness and the Comanche and still stood proud.

Dawson showed Matilda to a wing chair then made his way behind the desk to his own seat. Having the large piece of furniture between them would keep things at an impersonal level. Although what he had to say was about as personal as two people could get without actually touching, having Matilda out of reach for their conversation was very important to his frame of mind. Especially when what he really wanted to do was pull her body into his and take her mouth in a kiss hot enough to leave her panting and aroused and willing for whatever his body urged him to do.

Matilda sat, smoothing her skirt as she went. "What was it you needed to speak with me about in such a hurry, Mr. Chandler?"

Dawson was taken back for a moment. Not only did she appear irritated but her tone of voice was haughty, her pert little nose stuck in the air. It appeared as though she were looking down at him with eyes so dark he couldn't differentiate the pupils from the irises.

More than anything, he wanted to see her eyes widen with shock and then arousal before glazing over with lust and the overwhelming impact of a mind-numbing orgasm. He'd get at least a part of his wish by the time their conversation was over. That much he knew for sure.

"We've got much to talk about, Miss Cummings, but we'll start with the possibility of a marriage between the two of us."

"Possibility? I'm afraid I don't understand. From what Duncan said, the contract between us is binding."

Dawson could tell she was mulling something over. What he didn't know, however, was whether she was trying to find a way out of the contract or a way to keep to it.

"Yes, the contract in and of itself is binding but we have yet to share the marriage bed..." He purposefully let his words run off just to see what her next step would be. There was something about the expression on her cherubic face that intrigued him. She seemed smart and quick of wit. Being a woman to boot meant there was no telling what she was thinking.

Her full, dimpled cheeks pinkened even more. "Yes. Well, once we've said the words in front of a preacher, we can get to all of that."

Then she did the complete opposite of what he'd been expecting. Instead of fidgeting and twisting a lace hanky, as most ladies seemed to do when uncomfortable, she looked him in the eye. "I've actually been looking forward to our nights together."

From the expression on her face, the admission was a hard one. Dawson was immediately on guard, skeptical of what she could possibly know. Unless, she wasn't as innocent as she pretended to be.

Rising from his seat, Dawson walked around the desk until he was directly in front of Matilda. He knelt before her and, with a hand braced on each arm of the chair she occupied, leaned in close. He was close enough he could feel the warm puffs of her breath on his face.

"You have, have you?"

She audibly swallowed, her lips parting as if in need of more air as she nodded. "My...uh, my mother explained what would be expected of me."

Dawson couldn't help but chuckle. Her mother's explanation of sex more than likely had very little to do with the way things would go in their marriage, if they were indeed to go through with the services. Before taking any agreement on her part to heart, she would have to know everything.

Matilda seemed to be affronted by his laughter. Her obsidian eyes narrowed on him. Her lips clamped into a straight line resembling nothing of their full lusciousness.

"Don't get riled up, darlin'." Dawson rubbed the fullness of her cheek with the back of his hand. Her skin was soft and so warm she would surely burn him alive if he ever got the chance to sink the full length of his cock between her thighs.

For a second she seemed to melt into his touch. Dawson recognized the moment she came back to her senses for her spine stiffened and she turned away from his touch. "Do you wish me for a wife, Mr. Chandler? Your brother explained the predicament he'd placed you in so I'll understand if you feel the need to back out of the contract."

Dawson no more wanted a wife than he did a hole in his head but he had signed the contract and did feel somewhat responsible for the woman sitting before him. Because his honor was everything, Dawson would marry her but not until she knew exactly what she was getting herself into.

"I didn't wish for anyone as a wife, Miss Cummings, so please don't take what has happened personally. Duncan, in his infinite wisdom, saw fit to take my choices from me so we'll make the best out of the situation, if you decide to go through with becoming my wife."

A look of utter confusion clouded her face. His plan was to be blunt and to the point leaving nothing out. However, the way she tilted her head studying him nearly drove Dawson mad with lust.

"If you become my wife, Miss Cummings, things will never be between us the way your mother explained. Not only will you be my wife, you will be my lover in every sense of the word. You will, of course, act the lady you are except when it comes to our times together. In those instances, you will be as lusty as the best whore out there."

She raised a plump hand to her chest and clutched at the locket that hung nearly to her breasts. Her lips parted and her cheeks flushed. She looked appalled and excited all at the same time.

"I won't allow quick fumbles between the sheets in the dark. Do you understand what I am saying, Miss Cummings? If you become my wife, you will attend me, on my whim, wherever and however I see fit."

There. It was out. Dawson backed away from Matilda allowing her room to think, to breathe. With his luck, she would bolt or wilt to the floor in a fit of hysterics. What he had not prepared himself for was her next words, words she whispered in a voice so low and husky he almost came in his pants just hearing it.

"I think we'll suit, Mr. Chandler, but your impassioned speech makes me wonder exactly what I'll be getting out of this arrangement."

Chapter Three

It had been two of the most nerve-wracking days Matilda could remember ever experiencing. She couldn't seem to get the talk between Dawson and herself out of her mind. The way he'd leaned into her, bringing his mouth so close to hers she could almost taste his breath, had virtually stole her own.

Matilda still couldn't imagine where she'd worked up the nerve to ask him such a question. Indeed! *What would she be getting?* Was she crazy? It wasn't as if she expected more than knowing she would be marrying a stable, hard-working man who would treat her kindly.

His answering words still had the ability to make her tingle all over. "Pleasure, darlin'. Pleasure like nothing you've ever before or will ever again experience with any other man but me."

The fierceness of his kiss, when he'd ground his lips to hers, just about overwhelmed Matilda's senses. Warm and hard, his lips punished and took, leaving her mouth burning with fire. When she offered even more of herself, trusting her tongue against his in an entirely unknown way, Dawson gentled the kiss until his slow and thorough exploration of her mouth left Matilda breathless and dizzy.

Everything about this man screamed for her to run. He was large and overbearing and if she wasn't careful, very careful, she would forget where she ended and he began, ending up only a shell of herself.

Matilda shrugged the thought away. She would become Mrs. Dawson Chandler in a few days. Evidently Duncan had seen fit to make arrangements for a preacher to leave Dodge City several days after their departure, which was a good thing since Matilda had no plans to put the cart before the horse.

And from the looks of Dawson, whom she had been trying to avoid at all costs, the preacher had better hurry. Every time she was in his presence the hunger in his eyes bore through her until her insides felt jittery.

Thoughts of her soon-to-be-husband kept Matilda on edge, which meant she wasn't sleeping well. In return she'd wreaked all sorts of havoc, not only in the kitchen but while helping with the outdoor chores as well. The worst had been when, earlier in the day, she'd nearly gotten herself gored by a bull.

The episode was far from her fault. Dawson had taken it upon himself to corner her in a far stall of the barn, where he'd proceeded to kiss and touch her as if he owned her.

"I can't get the taste of you out of my mind, darlin'." He'd murmured the words against her neck, his voice dark and rough. It didn't matter how her body responded, immediately dampening her thighs, or how the feel of her nipples tightening against the confines of her corset made her ache from the inside out. What mattered was how he had the ability to render her senseless, a feeling Matilda didn't enjoy.

After kissing her breathless, Dawson had looked deep into her eyes. "Tonight, you'll come to my room." He must have been completely sure she wouldn't argue because in the next instant, he'd turned from her, leaving her to stand on jelly legs with only the abrasive wooden planks of the barn wall supporting her.

It took several minutes for Matilda to gather her wits enough to comprehend Dawson's command, at which time, she took off after him as if the hounds of hell were nipping at her heels.

As a grown woman, Matilda had no real reservations about sex. She might be a bit nervous, but she wasn't exactly clueless. On occasion, she'd taken pleasure in her own body, touching and experimenting, loving the release her fingers could pull from her own flesh and yet, she was not willing to go to her marriage bed without her innocence. Even if the man hell-bent on taking it was to be her husband.

With her mind in turmoil, Matilda hadn't realized Dawson had made his way into a corral, much less one housing a bull, or that by ducking through the wooden fence slats to follow him, she'd be putting herself in harm's way. Until the very large and extremely smelly animal had come charging at her, Matilda hadn't heard a single sound. She'd been so intent on catching up with Dawson and giving him a piece of her mind. After all, they weren't yet married so he had no reason to dictate to her.

Now, several hours later, Matilda scowled at the dish she was washing. After her little episode outside, Dawson had restricted her to the house where she was to attend to more ladylike activities. Just the thought of those condescending words and the equally condescending tone of voice he'd used made her want to bash him in the head with a blunt object. The big brute had even had the gall to suggest she sit beside one of the overly large windows and sew. Matilda couldn't help but roll her eyes and wonder just what she was getting herself into.

He hadn't yelled or cursed. His reaction was the complete opposite of what she'd expected. After rescuing her from the bull, he'd gone as still and quiet as a statue. Only his glittering green eyes gave away the extent of his anger and when he finally spoke, there was no denying just how mad he actually was.

"In the house, Matilda. Now. We'll talk about what happened after supper, in the privacy of my study." His growled words, low and rough, still had her a bit worried.

Supper was a tense affair. It seemed everyone at the table knew something was wrong and yet, nothing said or done had the ability to banish the thick shroud of discomfort from permeating the air.

Dawson sat rigid as he ate his evening meal while Duncan took the time to laugh and joke. Matilda had no clue how to act. She was angry at Dawson for making her uncomfortable but her anger wasn't geared only toward him, a fair share of it was aimed at herself. She'd acted like a complete ninny stalking off through the bull pen as if she didn't have a care in the world.

Under normal circumstances, she would have mulled over what to do next until she had every possibility played out in her mind.

For some reason, though, Dawson had the ability to render her speechless with no more than a look, and the mere touch of his lips upon hers left her senseless and aching for more. What in the world was she going to do when they finally made it to the marriage bed?

If what had transpired between them thus far was any indication, she would soon need instruction on the most simplest of tasks because evidently, when around Dawson, Matilda had no control over her emotions or reflexes.

She pushed the food around her plate without eating much, but it kept her hands occupied so she wouldn't wring them in a show of nervousness. It wasn't until Dawson placed a hand on her shoulder that she realized everyone had excused themselves from the table, leaving only Dawson and herself.

"Are you going to eat your supper or play with it?"

Matilda took his words as the challenge they were. Trying not to show the uncertainty coursing through her body, she dropped her fork and pushed her chair away from the table. "I'm finished."

When Matilda gathered her plate and headed toward the sink Dawson grasped her wrist, stopping her. "Just leave it in the sink."

Matilda was incensed by the thought of leaving Jess more work. "I will not!"

She wanted more than anything to fist her hands on her hips to make her anger well-known but decided against it. Learning to choose her battles wisely was going to be harder than she'd originally thought.

Without a backward glance at Dawson, Matilda began to pump water into the wash basin. Then, with more vigor than required, she scraped the leftovers into the slop bucket before scrubbing the plate as well as her fork.

It took no more than five minutes to complete the task. At the moment, she wished for a full sink of dishes to wash. Matilda rinsed out the washrag and wrung it as dry as she could before draping it over the edge of the sink. She was just reaching for the wash basin, when Dawson's hands covered her own.

"You've done your share. Come on, now."

With the ease of a man used to getting his way, Dawson led her from the kitchen. The feel of his fingers wrapped tightly, yet gently, around her wrist made Matilda's steps falter. His flesh was warm and made her tingle in a carnal way. Never before had she thought it possible a simple touch on her hand could cause heat to zing straight to her core.

She was a spitfire, a troublemaker of the worst kind. The way she smiled serenely even when her unease was clearly evident caused Dawson's lips to twitch. Her fire and innocence battled against each other, a battle he enjoyed watching.

It amused Dawson how Matilda seemed to have a bit of trouble holding her temper around him. He wasn't sure just yet if her bad humor was a good thing or a bad thing for their future, but before the night was over, he'd sure as hell be experiencing a bit more of it. Dawson was still irate over her carelessness earlier in the day. Had she already been his wife, Dawson would have taken great pleasure in paddling her ass and teaching her the error of her ways. But as things stood now, he'd do nothing but scare her off if he did so.

Although he'd originally thought he had no use for a wife, the sweet taste of her lingering on his lips proved being shackled might not be such a horrible plight after all.

After a short trip up the hall, they reached the study. Dawson used his free hand to open the door while still holding Matilda's wrist in the grasp of the other. Once in the room, with the door tightly closed, Dawson led Matilda to the same wing chair she had occupied on her last visit to the room. This time, though, he didn't use the desk to separate them. This time, he wanted to stay close to her.

Moving back, Dawson leaned a hip on the edge of the desk. With arms crossed over his chest, he gave Matilda his fiercest scowl. Instead of stumbling through an apology, as anyone in their right mind would when hit full force with his anger, she scowled right back.

The deep breath she took warned him she planned to start in on him, even before she opened her mouth. Dawson didn't plan to argue. He would point out the consequences of her actions and then it would be over. Then and only then would he be able to usher her off to the confines of his bedroom, the room they would soon share, where he could touch her pleasantly plump body and stroke the silky skin of her thighs before he buried his face between her slick folds.

After kissing her earlier today, Dawson had a fierce need to go further, to taste more. If her pussy was even half as sweet as he was sure it was, he might never come up for air. His shaft throbbed as visions of what her pale skin might look and taste like wormed their way through his mind. First though, he had to get through their talk and her coming to terms with what the punishment would be if she acted rashly again.

"So what do you have to say for yourself?"

She stared at him, her mouth slightly agape, as if he'd grown a third eye.

"You'll answer my question, Matilda."

This time her onyx eyes narrowed. "I would be glad to answer your question, Mr. Chandler, but I haven't a clue of what you are asking."

It took everything in Dawson not to move close and shake her silly. She had practically gotten herself maimed or even killed by Lucifer, the meanest son-of-a-bitch bull in the territory, and now, she acted as if she'd completely forgotten the incident. Her cool demeanor irritated him damn near as much as her use of his surname.

"I'm to be your husband. You'll call me Dawson." There, that should set her straight, he thought, trying with all his might to remain calm and in control. Such control was hard to master when what he really wanted to do was let her hair down and wrestle her out of her many layers of clothes. Thoughts of bending her over the polished surface of his desk before slamming the full length of his rigidly hard cock deep into her heated core just about brought Dawson to his knees.

"I believe Mr. Chandler is more to my liking. A least until we've traded vows."

Dawson searched Matilda's face for any sign of laughter, hoping she thought to joke with him instead of testing his patience but there was no lift to her lips, no twinkle to her eyes. She was indeed disagreeing with him, in his home, in the privacy of his study. Be damned! The woman was worse than a menace, she was infuriating.

Thinking to keep things on an even keel, Dawson calmly stated, "You call my brother by his given name."

Her cheeks pinkened at his declaration and for a moment, Dawson felt blinding rage thinking she was remembering something that had happened between Duncan and her. It wasn't until she explained that he understood.

"Your brother, although seemingly relaxed, can be very intimidating when he puts his mind to it."

Dawson was well aware Duncan, who was always ready with a smile, could be unforgiving and ruthless when provoked.

"If insistence is what is needed to prompt you into calling me by my given name, then I insist. You'll call me Dawson and think no more of it."

Was he going to have to spell everything out for the woman? If so, his days would prove to be very long. A jerky nod as well as the tightly clamped line of her lips spoke not only of her agreement, but her exasperation.

"Now back to my original questions. How do you explain nearly getting yourself killed today?"

Her voice was heavy with sarcasm when she answered. "Evidently I wasn't paying attention. I'm curious about your explanation though. How do you explain nearly attacking a woman, future wife or not, and then commanding her to your bedroom?" A deep well of emotions crossed her face, pulling Dawson into her dark gaze. "You took without permission what was not offered in the first place and then just left me."

Dawson wondered if his leaving was actually the crux of the problem or had he pushed too hard, too fast?

Her eyes now blazed with anger. "You want a whore for a wife in the bedroom? I can deal with that but we are as of yet unmarried and were not even close to a bedroom. In the future, I'd appreciate it if you'd learn to control your urges, Mr.…Dawson."

Pushing away from the desk, Dawson moved closer. "I have never attacked or nearly attacked a woman, Maddie. To say so would be the worst of insults." He kept his voice low as he loomed over her.

Her eyes widened at the use of the nickname he'd used many times in his head, while thinking of her, dreaming about the fullness of her pink lips stretched tightly around the head of his cock.

Dawson reached out and hauled her from the chair. The force of his movement sent her body careening into his chest. Maddie merely stared at him tongue-tied, when he held her at arm's length.

"And if I remember correctly, I said once you were my wife, I would have you on my whim wherever and however I see fit. I haven't changed my mind, darlin', but if coming to our bed a virgin is important to you, then we'll wait on that account, but only that one, Maddie. There's nothing saying I can't pleasure you or me in so many other wicked ways until the preacher makes it here."

Dawson lifted her from her feet. With swift and sure movements, he turned to the desk, where he settled Maddie onto its surface. "Tell me you want my touch."

She shook her head even as her arms remained wrapped around his neck, refusing to let go. Dawson grasped her wrists, unwinding her arms.

"Shhh," he crooned. "Don't tell me no, Maddie. Not when your pussy is probably slick for my touch. Should I check, darlin'? Should I see if you're wet for me?"

Her eyes were wide, bright with excitement and fear of the unknown. Her dimpled cheeks flushed, shining with a fine sheen of perspiration. She acted as though it was impossible to stay still, wiggling her round ass on his desk as if searching for release.

Dawson spread her legs with a hand on each knee and lifted her skirts then stepped into the void he'd just created. Maddie gasped.

"Say my name, baby. Say my name and tell me you want me to taste the sweet spot between your thighs."

When she remained silent, Dawson wound a hand in her hair and tilted her face up until their gazes locked. "Tell me." His words were whispered against her mouth. When he traced the seam of her lips with the tip of his tongue, Maddie relented, saying exactly what he'd longed to hear.

"Dawson."

His name on her lips, followed by a whimper of need as she tried to move closer, nearly blinded him with lust.

Chapter Four

His name rolled off her tongue, tasting sexy and natural. So natural, Matilda repeated it over and over in her head. The way he touched her with his work-roughened hands, commanding her to do his bidding, left Matilda feeling vulnerable and empowered all at the same time.

Since first meeting Dawson, she had longed to run her fingers through the wavy lengths of his hair. When he bent toward her chest to unfasten the row of buttons keeping her bodice closed, Matilda had the chance to do so. The dark wavy locks were much softer than they appeared. The way they twisted around her fingers, caressing her flesh, left goose bumps behind.

When Dawson lowered his head and traced the half moon of her areola as it peeked from above her corset, Matilda gasped at the pleasure then allowed the breath to hiss out of her over-inflated lungs.

One of his hands was once again busy beneath her skirt. This time he went further than merely parting her knees. To her utter excitement and mortification, Dawson walked his fingers up her thigh until he found the opening in her split drawers.

His fingers were magic, sending sparks of desire spiraling throughout her body in a way that left her completely breathless and aching for more. Her system was overloaded with sensation unlike any she had ever before experienced. The feel of his thick finger as it rubbed along her slit was nothing at all like the times she'd tentatively touched herself.

Matilda gave an involuntary shudder of delight when Dawson lowered himself to the floor in front of her. Without even removing her underthings, he plastered his face to the apex of her thighs. The very first swipe of his tongue caused her legs to tremble and her heart to pound against her ribs.

"Watch me taste you, Maddie. Watch me give you a bit of the pleasure I promised."

It was utterly impossible to ignore the command in his voice. Matilda tried not to think about the impropriety of her position or how tawdry she felt with her skirts around her waist and a man between her legs. Embarrassment threatened to overwhelm her just as the thrust of Dawson's tongue on her slick flesh did.

She hung precariously on the edge as he nibbled and sucked the most sensitive part of her. Matilda didn't realize she'd closed her eyes until all at once everything stopped.

"What?" She looked down only to find Dawson staring back at her, his green eyes intent, his brows drawn together in a displeased scowl. How could he be so cruel as to pull away when she was so close? Until the exact moment she'd began to voice her displeasure, Matilda didn't realize she still held Dawson's hair in the tight grip of her fingers.

When the realization slammed into her, Matilda dropped her hands from his head and looked at them as if they had just recently sprouted from her body.

"I, I…" Not one to stutter or back down from a challenge, Matilda was doubly mortified by her actions. With every intention of removing herself from Dawson's desk and, after righting her clothes, from his study, she pushed herself back and tried to scoot to the opposite side of the desk.

A ham-sized hand belonging to Dawson, who was still kneeling between her legs, stopped her movement with little effort.

"Where do you think you're going?" The controlled tone of his voice caused Matilda to shiver as did the way his lips glistened with her juices. Without giving her time to answer, Dawson spoke again. "Until I give you leave, you'll stay right where I put you while I give you pleasure so great you'll be overcome by it." He dipped low until his mouth hovered over her sex, his breath warm against her center, before growling, "And you will watch, Maddie, because you can't help but to."

He was arrogant and bossy and as much as she didn't want to admit it, he was absolutely right. It was as if he could see right inside of her, see the dark little corner of desire she kept secret.

He was a large man. Larger than any she'd ever seen with fists capable of crushing a woman with little effort. The width of his massive chest stretched the fabric of his shirt taut even as the muscles of his forearms spoke of hard work and strength. If he was so large, from head to toe, then surely that part of him, the part she'd only ever heard about between fits of giggles while with friends, would be large as well.

Being the maiden she was, Matilda should have been frantic with fear or at the very least, worried. After all, he was a man, who in a matter of days would own her the way a man owned any other possession. Only she wasn't afraid. Matilda was excited and nervous.

Dawson kept his grip firm on her one leg while grasping the other in the same manner. "Hold on to the desk, Maddie."

Matilda wasn't quite sure why she would need to hold on to the desk. It wasn't as if she might fall off, especially with his hands holding her firm against the smooth, polished surface but she did as he asked. His hold and the firmness in his voice brooked no argument.

After the first swipe of his tongue against her folds, Matilda gave up wondering why. In the next few minutes, when her body tumbled over the precipice, a cry of devastating pleasure torn from her lips, she knew why.

The feel of the desk beneath her hands was the only thing to keep her grounded, the only thing to keep her from splintering off in a thousand different directions. Never before in her life had she felt release so strong, so all consuming.

Her inner muscles spasmed around nothing. The feeling of emptiness left Matilda aching for more even as her body slumped in satiation. Following what her body needed, she grasped Dawson by his hair and with all her might tugged him to his feet in front of her.

Dawson's chuckle sounded more like a growl as he circled her waist with his muscular arms. Matilda, who had only one thing on her mind, fought his hold until her hand was free, free to seek the thickness pressing against the front of his trousers. She wanted to feel him in her hand, in her body and even against her tongue, if it was permitted. All thought of remaining a virgin until her wedding night fled. At the moment, Matilda would sell her soul to the devil himself for more.

"Oh please, Dawson. I need—" Matilda's plea was cut short by someone pounding on the door.

"Damn!" Dawson's voice sounded strained, on edge. He spat a few more select curses before finally moving away from her. "This damn well better be good." His bellowed words echoed throughout the room, cooling Matilda's ardor as fast as a bucket of cold water would have.

When she tried to move, Dawson pierced her with a determined look. "Stay! Right where you are."

She could have been a dog for all the emotion he put into the command. Matilda lowered her skirt, smoothing it the best she could. With trembling fingers, she began buttoning her bodice. It felt completely wrong to be perched on the edge of his desk, reminding her of what she had nearly begged Dawson to do to her, with her.

"The preacher's here." Jess's words were muffled by the closed study door.

Those three words had Matilda scrambling from the surface of the desk in unladylike recklessness and against Dawson's command.

"'Bout damn time." Dawson's words weren't so bad but the look on his face, in his glittering green eyes, was that of an animal on the prowl, ready to pounce upon its mate, to brand her and mark her as his. Matilda couldn't tear her gaze away from his even as she backed toward the door. Her cheeks aflame as she finally turned and fled the room passed a stunned Jess.

Dawson wasn't sure whether to strangle the preacher or kiss him. His interruption was very timely. If he hadn't shown up when he did, Dawson may have very well gone against his word and took Matilda right there on his desk, with her clothes still on.

Although already late, Dawson spoke with Jess and Duncan, as well as the preacher, who would be their guest for a few days, about wedding plans. He and Matilda would be married tomorrow afternoon with only Duncan, Jess and a few ranch hands present to share in the festivities. After being close to her, tasting her, there was no way in hell Dawson was going to wait any longer to make Matilda his wife.

Jess was all atwitter about the lack of time she had to get everything ready but Dawson couldn't bring himself to care about the preparations. He had no idea what "everything" entailed. All he knew was he didn't need anything fancy to make Matilda his wife. After making sure the preacher was comfortably set in a room of his own, Dawson made his way up the hall, on silent feet, to his room where Matilda was supposed to be.

Of course, where she was supposed to be and where she was were two completely different things. The damned stubborn woman had a mind of her own. She evidently had not been spanked enough as a child. The thought sent a wickedly sensual visual through Dawson's mind, one that would surely cause a hell of a ruckus if the need ever arose to go through with such punishment.

Without a second thought to what he was doing, Dawson left his room and headed straight for Matilda's. She might be stubborn and set in her ways but he was incredibly determined and had no plans of backing down until he got exactly what he wanted.

She lay in her bed, staring at the ceiling when he entered quietly, without knocking. Seemingly deep in thought, it took a few seconds for her to take in the fact that he was there, standing in her room.

"What are you doing?" The question was a whispered accusation. Her gaze snapped to the now closed door behind him before traveling up his body and landing on his face. She looked so outraged it was hard to keep from smiling.

Damned if she wasn't cute with the sheets pulled high, tucked beneath her armpits and the high collar of her gown buttoned to the very top. Her dark hair was plaited with the thick braid pulled over her shoulder and rested across the generous swell of her breast.

Dawson couldn't wait until they were married, a complete change of direction for his thoughts compared to a few weeks ago when Duncan had spilled the beans about his mail-order bride plan.

He wanted to command her to remove every stitch of clothing as he watched. Once she was beneath him, he could love her every way known to man before pulling her against his body while they slept.

"I'm here because once again, you didn't listen, Maddie. I remember telling you you'd be in my room tonight."

She looked positively horrified bringing Dawson's anger to the forefront. "You can't mean it," she cried. "Not with the preacher here."

"I never waste my time saying words I don't mean. Soon enough you'll learn that. You'll also learn there will be consequences when you don't listen."

This time her face paled a bit even as she thrust her chin out in a show of bravery. "Now I suppose you're saying you'll beat me if I don't listen." She jumped from the warmth of her bed and made her way to the armoire where she retrieved an overlarge carpetbag. "If you think I'll marry you, knowing you plan to inflict pain upon my person, you are seriously deranged." As she spoke, Matilda began to haphazardly stuff the bag full of her belongings.

She was evidently braver than she was smart to insult him by insinuating he would ever cause her, or any woman, harm.

"I might put you over my knee, setting your ass on fire with the palm of my hand, did I think you deserved such punishment, but I would never, and I mean never, intentionally hurt you."

Matilda's cheeks turned the most vivid shade of red at his words. Her shoulders sagged, Dawson hoped in relief, as she set the half-full carpetbag back in the bottom of the armoire.

"I'll marry you then, just as we had planned." Matilda spoke the words low, in a near whisper. "And I apologize if I insulted you. It wasn't my plan at all. I just needed to be sure of what your intentions were."

Dawson grinned widely. "I never, for one minute, doubted you would marry me." It wasn't as if she had much of a choice. Even if she decided to back out now, he could still insist upon the ceremony, especially since she still hadn't admitted her perfidy to him. She was not the woman Duncan originally planned for him and hadn't bothered to admit as much. It was Dawson's one ace in the hole. He moved closer, until they were toe to toe and he could smell her sweet womanly scent.

Leaning in close, he kissed the curve of her neck. "You're apology is accepted." Dawson nipped the tender flesh where neck and shoulder met. When she gasped, Dawson closed in on her mouth. He slid his tongue home, tasting, devouring everything she offered then insisting upon more. "Now, we'll go to my room." He spoke the words low against her mouth as he tore his lips from hers.

Matilda tugged her hand in an effort to free it from his hold as he led her from the room. "We can't." Her hissed words filled the air directly behind him. Her ineffective tugging was becoming very irritating when all Dawson wanted to do was lie beside her, holding her, until she snuggled close and fell asleep.

"Hush now," he prompted, as he lifted her curvy frame over his shoulder. She remained quiet but there was nothing meek about her behavior as she thrashed around, kicking and pinching, trying to get him to release her.

Once behind the closed door of the master bedroom, Dawson landed a solid swat to her wriggling ass. His hand tingled with the contact and his cock swelled to life so fast he thought his knees would buckle.

As he lowered Matilda to her feet, Dawson spoke in a low rumble. "Don't say a word, Maddie. Just get in bed and let me hold you tonight. I'll make sure you are back in your room long before the preacher rises."

She stared at him for a moment, as if gauging his sincerity. She was going to be the death of him before they finally came to an understanding. Then, with only the slight nod, she turned and did as he asked.

Dawson took his time blowing out the kerosene lamp lighting his room. Before climbing into bed, he removed every stitch of clothing covering his body. He wanted, more than anything, to insist Matilda do the same but wouldn't do so, at least not tonight.

With the knowledge that tomorrow night he would be a married man, Dawson climbed into bed behind a very stiff Matilda. He pulled her into the curve of his body, ignoring her token protests when the rigid length of his shaft made its presence known.

"Relax, darlin'. Just relax and let me hold you."

A grin of satisfaction curved Dawson's mouth when Matilda snuggled against him. Within minutes, her breathing became deep and even, a small snore escaping her lips every time she exhaled.

Dawson drifted off to sleep in complete peace. For the first time ever, he wondered why he had been so dead set against marriage.

Chapter Five

Warm heavy breathing against her temple woke Matilda out of a dead sleep. Her eyes popped open of their own accord, taking in the prickly square chin belonging to a man, a man who surely should not be in her bed.

Before her brain engaged enough to stop the action, Matilda opened her mouth to scream. A large hand clamped firmly across her lips stopped the sound before it escaped. "Scream and everyone within earshot will be barging through the door."

His voice was rusty with sleep, rumbling up from deep in his chest. Dawson. Matilda breathed a sigh of relief, her mind finally grasping where she was and what was happening.

She mumbled incoherently behind the hand he still held across her mouth. He needed to move, to release her. Dawson's manly scent, the feel of him against her side, big and strong, was doing some serious damage to not only her nerves but her libido as well.

His closeness made her want to rub her body against his like a bitch in heat. He was far too potent to be so close this early in the morning. When he changed positions, moving until he lay atop of her, one leg thrown over her and his hard length against her thigh, Matilda thought she might spontaneously combust.

His gaze was heavy lidded, traveling over her face in a thorough inspection. "I'll let you go if you promise not to scream."

Matilda nodded and was at once released. "Thank you."

Dawson's lips curved. "Ever the polite one." After a quick kiss to the tip of her nose, he levered himself off her until he sat on the side of the bed. "Time to go back to your room."

Matilda's gaze darted to the window at his words. She breathed a sigh of relief at the darkness beyond the glass. Without a word, she crawled from the bed, cursing the unladylike position the movement placed her in. Matilda was nearly to the door before Dawson called her back.

"We'll be married today." His brows creased and a strange look crossed his face. "Have you a special dress to wear?"

He didn't sound overly enthused by the prospect of marrying her. Matilda tried not to let the knowledge upset her. She would be a good wife and hope that over time, Dawson could form some sort of affection toward her.

"Yes, my mother insisted. It was the one thing she wasn't willing to compromise on."

Dawson stood. After wrapping the sheet around his hips, he walked across the room toward her.

"Good. Very good. I've got some things to do this morning but I'll be back for the noontime meal so there will be plenty of time to clean up before the ceremony."

He seemed uncomfortable about something, unused to explaining himself or his whereabouts more than likely. Matilda stared up into his face for a brief moment. It was impossible to ignore the need she had to show him things would be okay.

Allowing herself no second thoughts, she stretched up on tiptoe to kiss his jaw. With his great height and evident unwillingness to lower his face for her kiss, Matilda was left no other choice of where to place her lips.

Had she been too forward or done something to anger him? Damn, being a lady all the time sure was proving to be too much to work through on a daily basis.

She opened the door and quietly fled into the darkened hallway. Too tired to go back to sleep once in her own room, Matilda opened the trunk containing some of her belongings. Among the things still in the trunk was the wedding dress her mother had had commissioned for her.

She could hardly wait to wear it and yet it seemed almost out of place in the high prairie grasses of the public land strip, a place the Chandler family had called home for many years.

From what she'd heard, the area had no one to enforce the law. Some even referred to the public land strip as No Man's Land since it had been turned over by the state of Texas but was yet to be surveyed and allotted in a land run by the United States. And being so close to Indian Territory, Matilda wasn't quite sure just how many folks would choose the land as their home when and if it ever was split into parcels.

Jess had mentioned how Dawson's grandfather had settled the land long before the Comanche were sent to live on reservations, a time when war between the whites and Indians was prevalent. Matilda shuddered just thinking about the hardships both the whites and the Indians suffered through during that time.

No longer wanting to dwell on the bad, Matilda took her wedding dress from the bottom of the trunk, unwrapping it from the fine linen sheets it had been wrapped in.

The deep plum color of the dress did wonderful things for her pale complexion her mother had said. Matilda was just glad the one piece dress, with its fitted bodice, buttoned up the front so she wouldn't have to be too much of a bother come time to dress.

She idly ran a finger over one of the velvet-covered buttons as she held the dress to her body, eyeing herself in the mirror. The high neck and long sleeves were demure but the tightness of the garment would leave little doubt about her assets. Never one to be overly concerned about her plumpness or the over average size of her chest, Matilda felt a bit uneasy knowing Dawson would see her in the nude tonight.

Would he insist upon undressing her completely or would he settle for her merely lifting her nightdress and taking what he wanted. Somehow, Matilda didn't think so. Shaking all thoughts of her wedding night aside, she once again concentrated on the task at hand.

All the pleats and fringe would be hell to iron. Hopefully all that was needed to settle some of the wrinkles was a stiff shaking and the weight of the heavy skirts pulling at it while it hung.

Maggie Casper

By the time Matilda finished hanging the dress, as well as removing the rest of the items from the trunk, the day had broke. Sunshine spilled through the window of her room leaving in its wake warmth and comfort. Making her way down the stairs and into the kitchen, Matilda made a mental list of things she would need to do before afternoon arrived.

Several hours later, as she prepared for the ceremony, she prayed the large breakfast she'd eaten would stay down. Her stomach was in knots and had been for the past several hours but she was finally dressed and ready.

Matilda tucked the beautifully edged hankie Jess had loaned her into the top of her corset, happy she had everything she needed. Her mother's locket, her dress, the borrowed hankie and baby blue ribbon securing her chemise, not to mention the coin even now sticking to the side of her foot all made up the things Matilda needed to start her marriage off on the right foot.

Her hair had been arranged beautifully in an upsweep with long curls left to fall down her back. Jess had insisted upon threading wild flowers through the hair piled on her head, a time-consuming task Matilda was nevertheless grateful for. Her dress looked and fit perfectly, and on all outward accounts, she was calm and ready to face her new life as wife to Dawson Chandler, a man she still knew next to nothing about.

As she stood next to Dawson and faced the preacher, her whole body shaking and in turmoil, Matilda wondered for the millionth time just what in the hell she was getting herself into.

Dawson still felt breathless. His heart skipped a beat the moment Matilda walked into the room. Her pale face seemed even paler, her nervousness palpable. The full bow of her lips was berry pink and although exquisite, it was the contrast between her porcelain complexion and the deep raven of her hair as it spilled over the high neckline of her dress, which had his cock throbbing to life.

The deep purple dress she'd chosen to wear covered nearly every inch of her skin and yet, it left little to the imagination. The way it flared at the hips made her corseted waist appear even smaller, especially with the heavy weight of her breasts being lifted, as if in offering, by the binding garment.

Her neck was bare and graceful, beckoning Dawson to lick and nibble. It was a good thing the ceremony was short and only a small supper had been planned since those in attendance wouldn't be able to stay. Dawson was afraid if things stretched on, he was going to end up either making an ass out of himself or alienating his new wife by carrying her off before they even made it to dessert.

CR80

Later that night, Dawson watched as Matilda undressed before him, just as he'd commanded. The trembling of her hands as she did as he requested, no questions asked, endeared her to him all the more. She was willful and stubborn while at the same time, soft and womanly in a way he would know firsthand very soon.

When the dress lay pooled at her feet, leaving her clad in a long chemise covered by a beautifully edged corset and silk stockings, Dawson sucked in a breath.

"Breathtaking." The softly spoken word caused Matilda's cheeks to flush a becoming shade of pink.

He moved closer, slipping the buttons of his shirt loose from their moorings one by one. Without touching, Dawson circled Matilda, getting a close look at her pale flesh as it was being exposed inch by glorious inch. The sigh of relief that escaped her lips when she loosened and then removed her corset, freeing her bound breasts, caused his already aroused shaft to weep with need.

When Matilda reached for the blue ribbon tie at the neck of her chemise, Dawson stopped her.

"I'll do the rest."

Without waiting for her agreement, he ever so slowly pulled the blue ribbon until the neckline of the nearly sheer garment eased away from her body. Dawson's need was fierce when he tugged it off her upper body, trapping her arms in the process.

The sight of her heavy breasts spilling over the top of the filmy fabric left him no choice but to take her puckered nipple into his mouth. Matilda's startled gasp inflamed him in ways he'd never before felt. When she pushed against him, Dawson growled low in his throat. "Stay where you are, Maddie. Stay still and feel."

Dawson's words had the desired affect until he gave in to the urge to close his teeth against the tasty morsel, adding a bit of pain to her pleasure, hoping like hell she enjoyed the combination.

"Dawson?"

He backed off on the tension, noticing her every reaction, learning her body, her limits, in the process.

"Oh God. Oh yes. Please."

Did she have any idea she was begging? Asking for what she needed in a way so basic, so primal, even the deaf could understand the deep-seated need rolling off her body.

"Please what, darlin'?" Dawson wanted to hear her say the words. Pushing her chemise over her hips and to the floor, leaving her clad only in the silk of her stockings, made the need even greater. No longer buttoned up to her chin, Matilda had nothing to hide beneath. Nothing to remind her she was a prim and proper lady.

As she was, completely and gloriously nude, except for the sheerest of silk covering the generous curves of her legs, she would be his wife in ways she never could have imagined.

Dawson led Matilda to the bed in what was now their room. Once he settled her on her back, with his full length atop her, his weight held off only by the strength of one arm, he captured one of her peaked nipples between his fingers. Her hips bucked off the bed beneath him, her whimpered pleas echoing through the room astounding him at the sensualness running through the body of a virgin.

Adding a bit of pressure, Dawson repeated his question. "What is it you need, Maddie?"

Her eyes were glazed and heavy with lust. Her full lips were parted, a look of pleasure mingled with pain written clearly across her every feature.

"Do you want me to touch you, to take you?"

"Yes." Her tentative answer was whispered almost shyly. "Yes, please." He loved the sound of those words on her lips.

Dawson continued to play her body. He took turns capturing her nipples, first one and then the other while he teasingly worked the length of a single finger through the thick curls covering her slick folds. He leaned in, taking Matilda's lips in a searing kiss. When Dawson finally forced his mouth from hers, he levered himself off her enough to strip the silk stockings from her legs. Then, as a show of the mastery he loved to wield over the women he took to his bed, he lifted Matilda's hands over her head and loosely wrapped her wrists together.

The bonds would by no means hold her if she wished to be free but they would give her a clear idea of exactly what he'd meant when he'd warned her of his sexual preferences. "Keep your hands just as I've placed them. Do you understand?"

She undulated beneath him, her body slick and warm, covered in a fine sheen or perspiration. "I do. Just…please touch me."

It was impossible for Dawson to ignore such an invitation. Knowing firsthand just how wet and ready she was, he wedged his knees between her legs, spreading her thighs as wide as they would go before entering her in slow yet sure increments.

"So wet and hot. So damned tight." He groaned the words against her temple, having trouble holding back. Dawson had never before lain with a woman he claimed as his own, or a virgin for that matter. The thought of hurting Matilda haunted his every move.

He reached the evidence of her innocence and cursed, closing his eyes tightly against the pain he knew he would cause. When Matilda shook a hand free of her faux binds and cupped his face, he wasn't sure whether to reprimand her or thank her. Whatever Dawson decided on would have to wait. Her ragged pleas for more combined with the thrust of her hips, burying him just a little deeper, had all thought fleeing his mind.

With the finesse born of a stag in heat, Dawson plowed through her virgin's barrier until he was seated balls deep in her hot little pussy.

Matilda's sharp cry of pain at his possession was soon replaced by lusty moans, sounds so all consuming Dawson wasn't sure he'd ever be able to stop thrusting his length into her wet core.

She continued touching his face and writhing beneath him until Dawson felt as if he would explode. "I'm never going to make it, darlin'." He powered into her heated depths, the vise-tight grasp of her sheath rendering him helpless. "Come for me, baby. Let me see you fly."

Dawson's command was murmured gruffly against her ear as he reached between them to apply pressure to her clit. "Now, Maddie. Now!" With two more deep thrusts, her pussy contracted and rippled, sucking his length and milking him dry. Dawson shouted his release before collapsing atop her pliant body in an exhausted heap.

Chapter Six

Matilda waded through the chicken coop and its numerous occupants to retrieve eggs. It was one of the few chores Dawson allowed her to help with. For some reason the highhanded ogre thought her too addlebrained to accomplish much on her own.

It wasn't her fault she had a penchant for getting herself into trouble. She wasn't used to living on a ranch or the work involved. She needed someone to teach her. Up until traveling west, Matilda's most strenuous job was remembering to be a lady. Just the thought of going back to wearing all that frippery, when she'd been married three weeks and hadn't donned a corset for two of them, was enough to make her queasy.

Dawson might very well be an overbearing oaf at times, but he had the ability to make her hot and wet with no more than a look. He actually enjoyed her curves and had been thrilled the first day she'd dressed without donning a corset. Of course, in doing so, she'd created a monster, one set on having her anyway and anywhere he saw fit.

The wicked things he'd done to her willing body, and asked of her in return, had the ability to make her blush from head to toe and pray even harder on Sunday.

Something moving along the ground brought Matilda's wicked thoughts to a screeching halt. She was sucking in a lungful of air in preparation to scream her head off when she recognized the varmint for what it was. A gopher snake.

The scream died on her lips a low moan. It had only been a few days since her last chicken coop incident and she wasn't about to have a repeat, no matter how afraid of the legless creature she was. Screaming at the sight of a harmless gopher snake, in turn bringing half the ranch, including Dawson and Duncan running, would accomplish nothing except to get her restricted to the house once again.

"Not this time." Matilda muttered the words, hoping the conviction in her voice would work its way through her system. "It's harmless, Matilda. Just do it."

Allowing herself no time to balk, Matilda set her egg bucket down. She pulled one of the stout branches serving as a roost from its resting place then proceeded to lift the snake off the ground.

It stared at her with its beady black eyes and flicked its tongue, something Matilda tried to block out. She felt as though her skin was crawling. Fear coursed through her veins as the thing slithered a small ways up the stick but Matilda refused to let it scare her into putting it down.

"I've finally got a chore all my own. I won't let you eat my eggs, you ghastly beast." It wasn't until Matilda backed out the door of the coop, the stick held as far as possible in front of her, that she realized the snake was making a God awful racket with its tail, something she didn't remember the gopher snake doing.

"Oh shit!"

Matilda swiveled her head around to see Dennis, one of the Rocking C's ranch hands staring at her. He pushed his hat off his forehead. "Put the stick down, ma'am. Nice and slow."

Something about the tone of his voice had Matilda lowering the end of the stick just the slightest bit. Her action had the noisy snake moving further up its length. By this time, Dennis was pale and moving steadily back toward the barn. "Shit! Shit! Shit! Hold the stick still, ma'am. Don't lower it no more."

"Would you make up your mind, Mr. Bonner? You're starting to make me nervous." It was the first time since coming to the decision to eradicate the chicken coop of the snake that Matilda wondered if she'd made a grievous mistake.

"Lou. Call the boss." Dennis stayed out of reach but kept his eyes trained on the snake perched halfway up her stick.

Those words had the ability to make Matilda pale as well. Why did they have to bring Dawson into the picture? She was taking care of everything just fine without his help. "That isn't necessary, really Mr. Bonner. I'm just going to take this little guy out back to the garden and collect my eggs as normal. There really is no reason to fetch Mr. Chandler."

She'd barely finished the sentence when Dawson rounded the corner of the barn at a dead run. It was amazing how quickly he could move for such a large man.

"What's going..." Dawson bellowed what Matilda was sure would have been a demand to know what was going on just before his eyes landed on her. "Good God."

His usually sun-bronzed skin turned a sickly gray. It wasn't until then Matilda began to worry. He wasn't ranting or raving, he was worried or ill. She eyed the snake then Dawson and her hands began to shake.

"Please tell me this is a harmless gopher snake?" Her question ended on a high-pitched shriek.

"Stay still, Maddie."

Matilda grasped the stick with her other hand, hoping that by holding it with both, it might stop the shaking. "Tell me this is a gopher snake, Dawson!" She was feeling a bit hysterical when a voice sounded behind her.

"Close your eyes and stand very still, Matilda." It was Duncan. She wanted to turn and see what he was doing but Dawson chose that moment to growl at her and from his tone, he meant to be obeyed. "Do as he says, Maddie."

A loud crack sounded at the same time the stick in her hand splintered. A strangled scream left her lips, leaving her hoarse with its intensity. Within seconds, she was in Dawson's arms, his mouth crushed to hers. Matilda was just enjoying the sensation, melting into his embrace, when he shook her hard enough to rattle her teeth.

"Damned fool!" His words were growled low, for her ears only. Dawson continued to mutter oaths as he dragged her toward the house.

Matilda struggled to keep up and when she stumbled, for the third time, he lifted her into his arms, cradling her close. For a minute, she thought he meant to take her to bed. Only the stiffness of every muscle in his body, as well as the clenching and unclenching of the muscle in his jaw told her otherwise. Instead, he carried her into the study and kicked the door closed behind them. Once inside, he stood Matilda on her feet. With his legs planted far apart, as if readying for battle, Dawson pierced her with his gaze.

He was angry, very angry, and Matilda wasn't exactly sure why.

"You're more trouble than you're worth." His words hurt and confused, causing her heart to sink. "That was a Goddamned rattler you were playing with, Maddie!"

Matilda put her hand to her brow, feeling a bit lightheaded and queasy. She was afraid it would turn out to be something equally horrible. "I didn't know. I thought it was a gopher snake." *And I wanted to make you proud by taking care of it myself.* She thought the latter but couldn't bring herself to say it out loud, especially now knowing the way he felt about her.

"A gopher snake! You…I…" Dawson couldn't seem to get the words out. His face mottled with rage and although Matilda didn't fear for her welfare, she knew he would mete out some sort of punishment.

He'd warned her after the last chicken coop incident that she was trying his patience. Evidently it was now gone. She could understand why he was irritated, even irate, but there was absolutely no reason to belittle her due to a mistake. She intended to say as much when Dawson thrust a finger in her direction.

"You're to stay in this house, Maddie, until I say otherwise. Use the time to sew some of the things I left in the mending basket for you." He moved away from her, toward the door.

"I'm tired of staying in this damned house." Matilda did something she'd never before done. Besides cursing out loud, she stomped her foot in pique.

Evidently Dawson was just as surprised by her outburst as she was because he strode back across the room until he nearly ran her over. Backing her to the desk, he leaned into her. Placing both hands flat on the desk, he very effectively trapped her.

"I'm going to go now, Maddie, before I do or say something I'll regret." His eyes glittered. Even when angry, her closeness affected him. Matilda had to fight the urge to use her body to get what she wanted. "But you will listen to what I just said."

Dawson levered himself away from her and backed away just far enough so they weren't touching. "Leave this house and there will be hell to pay, Maddie. Don't test me on this. You won't win." Then without another word, he strode from the room.

Matilda was so angry she saw red. "Hell and damnation!" Her language really was taking a turn for the worse but in her anger, she didn't care. Her mind whirled with a need to do something to show her independence, something to show Dawson he had no say in what she did.

Leaving the house was out. Matilda might be stubborn but she wasn't stupid. With a smile born of wicked intent, she stalked from the room and up the stairs to their bedroom where she pulled what she needed from her sewing basket. By tomorrow morning, Dawson Chandler would learn his wife was not to be taken lightly.

His body ached with fatigue but he wasn't ready to turn in for the night. Dawson speared another clump of soiled straw from the floor of the barn, anger still riding him. If he went back into the house before Matilda was asleep, he might very well throttle the little troublemaker. As it was, she needed a burning hot spanking, one that would remind her to be safe.

Every time he slowed down for a minute, Dawson heard the rattle and hiss of the snake as it sat perched on the stick Matilda held. Once Duncan had shot the snake, the only thing Dawson could think to do was pull Matilda into his arms. It wasn't until he was sure she was safe that his anger boiled over.

And in the process of being angry, he had said some hurtful words, could still see the knowledge in the memory of her dark, hurt-filled eyes. And instead of staying out long enough to cool off, he'd stayed out all day even going as far as missing supper and mucking stalls by lamplight.

He'd never pegged himself for a coward but there was something about Matilda, about the way she'd burrowed so deeply under his skin in such a short time that had him scared spitless.

When every light in the house had been doused and all the windows stood dark, Dawson made his way in. On silent feet, he shuffled around the kitchen and made a sandwich for himself from the covered plate of leftovers on the counter. Once finished, he washed up then headed up the stairs to bed.

When he entered the room, Matilda lay curled on her side. Instead of being nude, the way she knew he preferred, she wore a long chemise. Dawson wanted to strip it from her body and take her where she lay, but he wouldn't do it. She'd been through enough. Between the snake and their argument, she was probably exhausted.

Trying not to wake her, Dawson climbed beneath the covers and gently pulled Matilda into the curve of his body. She stiffened and mumbled something before relaxing once again. Within minutes she was emitting the daintiest of snores.

Knowing Matilda was safe, and with a plan to talk things over in the morning, Dawson let sleep take him.

CR80

Bright streams of sunlight woke Dawson the following morning. It was the first time since his youth he could remember sleeping past daybreak. Knowing he needed to make things right, Dawson reached for Matilda, intent on saying his piece and then lecturing her on how important her safety was to him. Instead, he grasped empty space and cool sheets.

Matilda was gone and had been gone for some time already. The thought brought him up short. There was no telling what the woman was up to or getting herself into. Dawson launched himself out of bed, taking in the room around him as he made his way to the chest of drawers where his clothes were kept.

Everything seemed to be in place, including Matilda's belongings, which meant he hadn't hurt her feelings enough to send her running. Dawson grabbed a pair of faded denims from the drawer as well as his favorite button-down shirt. If the shirt was back in his drawer then Matilda must have taken his advice to sew to heart. Dawson smiled in triumph as he headed back to the bed.

"What the hell." His growled words echoed off the wall as he tried, with no luck, to slip his foot through the leg of his pants. The damn thing was sewn together.

A thought too horrific to be true slithered through his mind. She wouldn't!

"She damned well did!" Dawson pawed through his meager belongings, noting how every single thing he owned had been, in some way shape or form, altered, and not for the best.

A few of his shirts had a sleeve sewed closed while others were sewn up the front so he couldn't get them unbuttoned. It was his pants she'd gotten clever with. Some had the legs sewn shut or to each other. One even had the opening for the foot sewed to the back pocket.

If Dawson wasn't running late, and already at the end of his patience with his willful wife, he might very well have laughed about what she'd done. But he was late and his patience was long gone as was his need to talk things through with her.

"Oh, we'll talk all right," Dawson grumbled, as he used his pocketknife to slice the stitches holding his clothes hostage. "We'll talk. Right after I leave my handprint all over her troublesome ass."

Once he was finally dressed, Dawson made his way down the stairs and into the kitchen.

"Morning, boss. You feeling all right?" Jess watched him, a twinkle in her eyes. Dawson would bet his best hat she knew exactly what he'd been upstairs doing.

"I'm fine," he drawled, his vexation evident in his tone.

He wanted to ask where Maddie had hidden herself but wasn't quite sure he was ready for the answer. He needed time to cool off, time to think about paddling her ass in a way that would bring his cock throbbing to life for some rough loving after. Right now, he was more apt to take her out back to the woodshed and let her feel the lash of his belt.

Breakfast was eaten in silence and when he felt he finally had control over his emotions, he asked Jess the question he'd been dying to ask since entering the kitchen.

"Where's Maddie taken herself off to this morning?"

Jess strolled her way across the kitchen, taking her time, irritating the hell out of Dawson in the process. "That gal of yours came down bright and early this morning wringing her hands something fierce. She refused breakfast and said she was going for a ride but would be back in a short while. I expect her any time now."

"God Almighty! That woman is going to be the death of me. Please tell me she had the good sense to take one of the hands with her?"

With her head cocked to the side, Jess studied him, a bit too long and a whole lot closer than Dawson was comfortable with. "If I understood her right, there was no reason. She was merely going for a short ride in the pasture behind the barn. Said Mr. Bonner told her it was clear of critters for the morning at least."

Dawson gave a curt nod to Jess, slapped his hat on his head and strode purposefully out the door. At least she'd seen fit to talk to someone before taking off. Hell, he hadn't even known she could ride. Being born and raised in the city didn't lend itself to riding, especially astride.

His steps ate up the ground between the house and the barn. He was intent on finding Dennis and checking out the story Jess had told him. Although he felt guilty for doing so, Dawson believed he'd been left no choice. He didn't trust Matilda to keep herself safe.

He'd just reached the corner of the barn when the thundering of horse's hooves met his ears and shook the ground beneath his boots. The next thing he heard was Matilda's laughter immediately before she streaked across the rolling pasture behind the barn atop Daisy, a loud paint he'd raised since birth.

They looked magnificent together—Matilda with her inky black hair billowing out behind her and Daisy with her white mane doing the same. Hunched over Daisy's neck, Matilda moved with her as if they were one.

When they slowed, Matilda patted Daisy's neck, her smile as bright as the sun. Although he was fairly sure she'd seen him, by the way her back went rigidly straight, she refused to acknowledge him. Without so much as a wave, Matilda turned Daisy and headed for the barn at a leisurely walk.

Upon reaching the barn, Matilda reined Daisy in to a full stop then dismounted. She spent the next thirty minutes unsaddling and grooming Daisy. She hummed softly as she did the chore, her voice sounding angelic. Dawson snorted at the thought. She blessed the horse with a beautiful smile before leading her back to her stall. Once finished, Matilda made her way out of the barn, her dark eyes meeting his, and frowned.

Dawson silently swore he'd take Matilda riding any damn time she wanted if she would only laugh and smile in his presence the way she was with Daisy. Of course, everything would have to wait until after he'd taken care of business. Dawson's hand tingled. His cock throbbed to life, making his jeans very uncomfortable. It was beyond time the little minx got what was coming to her.

Chapter Seven

Matilda knew she was pushing her luck but never before had misbehaving been so fun. Dawson was angry and it didn't scare her. Quite the contrary, it excited her beyond belief. So far, in their short marriage, he'd managed to hold himself back, never getting boiling mad or extremely passionate. He normally growled and grumbled and sent her to the house if he thought anything was amiss.

Although a very passionate man, he kept himself on a tight leash. Matilda saw it nightly in the green depth of his eyes. He held her as if she were breakable and needed extreme care. Not only resorting to confining her to the house in order to keep her safe but also touching her with reverence, timing his strokes as he moved within her, keeping the dark side of himself buried deep. The worst part was not knowing why he felt the need to hold himself back.

Oh how she wanted to bring the wild, animalistic side he kept hidden, out in him. It might not be proper to ask for or even admit to herself but she longed for what she knew Dawson was capable of giving. He could love her and attempt to tame her in a way so sensual they might never be the same again.

The only problem Matilda saw in her need for more in the bedroom was that by allowing Dawson even the tiniest bit more say over her, she was more than likely going to have to fight even harder for independence when it came to non-intimate matters. Maybe after her rebellious sewing escapade, he would finally understand.

Matilda had only taken a few steps through the barn doors past Dawson when she felt his hand on her shoulder. In the time it took her to take a breath, he had spun her around and upended her over his shoulder. His voiced "up you go" was her only warning as her world tilted.

She put on a good show of kicking and hitting his broad back, but deep down inside, she was thrilled by his actions. The ease in which he lifted and carried her left Matilda in awe at his strength for she was no skinny miss to be blown away by a slight breeze.

The spot between her legs was wet and hot, aching for his touch. Only the knowledge of Jess and the ranch hands seeing her in the precarious position Dawson had placed her made her even the slightest bit uncomfortable.

Unsure of what he had planned made her mind whirl. He was angry and had every right to be but there was much more going on, at least where she was concerned. Matilda took the time to study Dawson's back. Then moving her gaze down his tapered waist, she eyed the rock hard swell of his buttocks beneath the thick denim of his pants.

The bright red thread poking out of his shirt and pants brought a giggle bubbling from her lips. Matilda couldn't help but pluck the loose strands from his clothes. She still wasn't sure exactly what had come over her but whatever it had been, there was no going back now.

Dawson stalked through the open kitchen door only stopping long enough to talk to Jess. "My wife and I will be upstairs, we have a few things to work out."

He punctuated his words with a harsh smack to her upturned butt. It was a swat much harder than Matilda had ever experienced in her life, causing her bottom to heat and ache all at the same time.

Was a spanking what he had in store for her due to her impertinence? Would each swat be as harsh as the one he'd just landed? All thought fled her mind when Dawson added, "You might want to pack a picnic lunch for the men. This could prove to be long and loud."

Matilda was about to start struggling for real, wondering once again what she'd gotten herself into, when Dawson landed another well-aimed blow with his big hand. This time her gasp was audible.

Once in their room, Dawson placed Matilda on her feet then closed and locked the door. He pocketed the key, leaving her no escape, before removing his hat and hanging it on a hook beside the door.

Matilda spun away from him, unsure if she was still excited about pushing Dawson beyond his limits, only to notice all his clothes were stacked neatly on the bed, along with her sewing kit.

She should probably say something but had no idea what it might be. Besides, she wasn't really sorry for what she'd done, no matter how childish it was. Dawson saved her from mulling the situation over, more than likely giving herself a headache in the process.

"I don't want to hear any excuses or apologies. You evidently had your reasons for doing what you did and we'll talk about those later. Right now what I want you to do is to change out of those tight pants and into one of your dresses."

While his words lifted the weight from her shoulders in one way, in many others they angered her. Had she gone through all the trouble of showing her independence, riling his ire, only to be made to change? Once she was finished would he just leave her locked in the room while he went about his business? Surely not!

Matilda's gaze darted from the window to the bed, her mind already thinking of ways she could use the sheets to lower herself to the ground. She might be a woman, one who had a tendency toward trouble, but she would not be locked in her room like a nuisance child. Matilda spun on her booted heel, catching Dawson staring at her denim-clad ass in the process. His eyelids were lowered, his green eyes heated with desire. So, her pants had gotten his attention.

It was the first time she'd worn them since leaving home. Before now, she'd been entirely too scared by his reaction. This morning however, Matilda figured she was already in about as much trouble as she was going to get into so she might as well be comfortable while out riding.

"I'll get you some pants to wear but you're not to wear the ones you have on again." His jaw locked together, making Matilda wonder just what it was about the pants she was wearing that he didn't like.

Dawson walked passed her to the armoire where he rummaged through the top shelf. By the time he found what he was looking for, Matilda had shucked her pants and shirt and donned one of her everyday calico dresses. She was buttoning up the last few buttons when he spoke again.

"Leave the rest undone."

Dawson now stood close to her, his words clear, as was the command in his voice. Matilda faced him and waited to see what he would ask of her next. She was sure her face bore a mask of confusion.

Matilda didn't have long to wait. "Lift your skirt, Maddie. Tie it up nice and tight so it stays put."

The underlying sensuality of his words combined with the deep timbre of his voice captivated her until Matilda found herself doing as he asked over the increasingly rapid beat of her heart. In her hurry to change, she'd forgone a clean pair of drawers, leaving herself completely nude beneath the skirt of her dress, not even a petticoat in sight.

Imagining exactly how she looked to Dawson made Matilda's face heat. The bodice of her dress gaped open, exposing her unfettered breasts. The length of her skirt was lifted and tied, just as he'd asked, showing her bare thighs above the length of her striped cotton stockings. The only womanly frippery she had on was the ribbon tying her stockings in order to hold them up.

Up until this point, Matilda had stayed silent, almost afraid to push further but there was no way she could just stand there with all of her assets on display. "I umm… Why am I standing here like this?"

Dawson's brow drew together in an irritated frown. "Tell me, Maddie, when you got into trouble at home did the punishment fit the crime?"

His abrupt question threw her off guard. "I believe so." Matilda shrugged. It was hard to remember since she hadn't often been punished.

"Glad to hear it. We'll have no trouble getting through this then." Dawson set the box he held on the bedside table before moving toward the overlarge chair taking up one corner of the room.

It had a high back and high wide arms. Both were overstuffed and covered with velvety brocade so decadent and smooth, her fingers itched to touch it. It was more of a lounger than a chair and Matilda couldn't, for the life of her, picture Dawson sitting there watching her do whatever it was he'd concocted as her punishment.

"Choose one of the garments you altered as well as the small scissors from your sewing kit and come here."

Here it comes, Matilda thought. As requested, she chose a chambray shirt, one she'd sewed the wrists together on, forming a semicircle of the arms, and the scissors. The bright red stitches were large and easily visible. She hadn't been sewing for real, something needing tiny, blended in stitches. No, she had been making a point, a point she was now going to pay for.

Supplies in hand, with her bare breasts and nude sex completely on display, Matilda made her way to Dawson. Without a word, he bent her over the wide arm of the chair. Her precarious position caused her to rise on the tips of her toes.

The cool air of the room across her ass and the lips of her sex reminded Matilda just how exposed she was. The feel of Dawson's fingers gliding across her bare flesh only slammed the fact home.

"You'll fix every shirt and pants, one by one, while I spank your…"

"Oh God." Matilda's whispered words interrupted Dawson, earning her a stinging swat.

"…luscious ass. We'll continue every day until you've finished. Am I understood?"

Matilda gulped, sucking in a much-needed breath at his words. Had she heard him right? Every day? Bemoaning her impulsive behavior, she answered. "Yes, sir, I understand."

Her breathy words, the fact she'd called him "sir" had Dawson's cock standing at attention. She looked absolutely wanton bent over the chair. The pale globes of her ass, beckoning him, quivered with every tremble of her body.

Dawson wasn't at all sure how he would make it through her punishment but he would. The damned minx had made an ass out of him, pushing him beyond his limits. She deserved everything she got and Dawson had plenty to give.

"Go ahead and get started while I prepare the rest of your punishment, darlin'." He ended the gently phrased command with a peppering of swats to her ass, just enough to heat her pale flesh.

Her body visibly stiffened at his words, but Dawson had plans, ones he had no intention of backing down on. Since their wedding, he'd taken Matilda in about every way a man could take a woman, teaching and being taught in return.

Dawson had held his lustier side back, not wanting to scare Matilda or ask too much when she so willingly offered him everything. That all changed after her ornery behavior the night before. Now, he would hold nothing back.

With his back to her, Dawson opened the small wooden box he'd kept hidden in the top of the armoire. In it sat a stair-stepped set of sculpted wooden anal plugs covered in the softest of leather, ones he'd had made just for Matilda, and brought in from Dodge City not long after their wedding. A small tin of lubricating ointment also filled the box.

Thinking of what he had planned for his naughty wife sent fingers of awareness up his spine, causing his balls to draw closer to his body. Dawson palmed three of the varying sized anal plugs as well as the lubricant and made his way back to where Matilda was doing her best to fix his tortured shirt.

Dawson kept hold of the smallest plug while setting the other two where she could clearly see them. "Open your legs, Maddie."

Her dark eyes caught his attention as she peeked at him over her shoulder. Dawson kept his face blank, wanting to give away nothing of what he was feeling. When she obeyed his command, he ran a finger up the length of her slit, carrying the slick cream he found there up between her ass cheeks, just grazing the tight ring of muscle protecting her anal opening.

The breath she sucked in echoed throughout the room, letting Dawson know she'd read his intent correctly. On the next pass, his finger was coated with lubricant, allowing the tip to dip slightly deeper.

When she dropped the small scissors, Dawson smiled and retrieved them for her.

This time when Dawson fingered Matilda, sinking in to the first knuckle, reveling in the tight heat of her ass, he spanked her. The sound of flesh upon flesh, as his palm landed again and again, drowned out her cries. If she hadn't been thrusting her ass back at him, silently begging for more, Dawson would have worried he'd hurt her.

The pink cheeks of her ass were everything he could have imagined and more. "Get back to work, Maddie."

Dawson stopped spanking her then pulled his finger from her body. He prepared the plug he'd put in his pocket while fighting the urge to remove his clothes and take her over and over again.

Once the plug was generously lubricated, he stepped behind her. With his palm flat on her back, Dawson wedged a knee between her thighs, in the process, lifting her feet completely off the floor. In her current position, she was helpless and at his mercy.

"Dawson?"

"Keep working, Maddie. You've got a lot of stitches to remove." He peeked over her shoulder and couldn't help but chuckle at how little she'd managed to accomplish in the time since her punishment had begun. From the looks of it, the next several days were going to be a test in erotic punishment like none ever experienced before.

The way Dawson held her curvy ass high with his leg left his hands free. With the fingers of one, he parted her fleshy cheeks, loving the small moan escaping Matilda's lips at the action. With the other hand, he pressed the tapered tip of the anal plug to her puckered opening.

"I don't think…"

"Don't think, Maddie. Now take a deep breath and try and relax, it'll go easier for you."

The sight of her tiny puckered hole stretching to take the plug nearly had Dawson tumbling over the edge. Her breath hissed out from between her lips as the widest part slipped past the tight ring of muscle. When it was finally seated completely within her body, only the flared base visible, Dawson leaned forward, trapping her beneath him, to kiss her just below the ear.

"Good girl." He crooned the words while running his hand along the length of her spine.

"I'm done with your shirt."

Her low spoken words brought Dawson out of his lust-induced stupor, reminding him of why he was in the room with a nearly naked Matilda beneath him.

"Go fetch something else to fix then," he said, backing away from her luscious body. "I'll put this one back where it belongs." Dawson gathered the shirt from Matilda's trembling fingers.

Dawson watched Matilda make her way to the bed and back. Her movements were slow and uneasy due to the anal plug nestled firmly within the tight confines of her ass.

Dawson waited until she was once again settled over the arm of the chair before moving back to her. Then, with nothing more than his fingers sliding along her puffy nether lips, he brought her so close she was moaning and begging for more. How he loved the woman splayed before him, taking the punishment he greedily applied.

Love?

Dawson's head reeled. When in the hell had he fallen in love with his wife? The enormity of the emotions he was feeling nearly sent him to his knees. Did she love him as well?

Matilda's upper body moved beneath his hand, drawing his attention. She watched him over her shoulder. Her dark gaze fastened to his with such intensity his eyes burned with hope.

No longer able to hold onto his desire in the face of what he'd just learned about himself, Dawson ripped at the fly of his pants. Within seconds, he was nude from the waist down.

Without thought for anything else, he grasped Matilda's hips and thrust home. The anal plug still firmly lodged in her ass made her fist-tight pussy even tighter. The sound of air being forcibly expelled from her lungs as Dawson hammered into her, sending her upper body into the arm of the chair, is what finally brought him to his senses.

"God, baby." Dawson pulled back in an attempt to regain control.

"No!" Her words were high-pitched, desperate. "Don't leave. Don't leave me."

Dawson slowed his pace but kept his cock embedded deep within her. "I'm not going anywhere."

Her hips thrust back at him, nearly breaking the tenuous hold he'd regained on his control. "Don't hold back, Dawson. Love me. Love me hard the way I know you want to."

Dawson held still for a moment, unsure he'd heard her correctly. "Tell me what you want." The command in his voice could not be ignored. When she didn't answer, he swatted her ass hard, peppering the smooth globes until they were pink and hot. "Now, Maddie."

"Take me. Show me what you really want."

Matilda's words had just died on her lips when he lost it. Letting the dark side of himself free, Dawson plowed into her while rotating the flared base of the anal plug until she screamed her release.

The way her inner muscles clamped down on his cock, milking him from base to shaft, drug an orgasm of magnanimous proportions from his body. Never before, even with the most seasoned of whores, had he come as hard or as long as what his very own wife managed to drag out of him. There was no doubt about it, he was a lost cause, a man who would soon be wrapped around the little finger of Maddie Chandler, the most wonderfully irritating woman west of the Mississippi.

Chapter Eight

Matilda's body hummed with spent heat as Dawson snuggled her close to his chest and carried her to the bed. Feeling him let loose was all she could have imagined and more. She even missed the plug he'd so naughtily used as part of her punishment, as embarrassing as that was to admit even to herself.

"Why haven't you ever done that before?" Her voice was low, seeking the information she longed to know, yet fearful of breaking the wonderful, post-sexual haze lingering over them.

"What, darlin', spank you? Because until last night your actions hadn't warranted such consequences."

His gravelly chuckle ran along her flesh, reigniting her already sensitized nerve endings in the process. Matilda dug her elbow into his ribs just to let him know she wasn't completely tamed.

"You know very well that is not what I meant. I want to know why…well, uh…" Matilda swallowed past the knot of embarrassment clogging her throat then decided if they were to have a future and any kind of a real relationship within their marriage they would have to start talking.

"Why haven't you let go before? I know you've wanted to. I could see it in your eyes when you watch me as you move between my legs."

Dear Lord, she'd said it. Matilda was glad Dawson was at her back. Her cheeks must be fiery red. His shaft, which lay nestled between the cheeks of her bottom, stirred to life, making its presence known. Surely he couldn't be recovered all ready?

The resulting inferno flowing through Matilda's body took her by surprise. Just knowing her larger-than-fashionable body had the ability to affect him so swiftly made her feel strong. Empowered.

His voice, when he finally answered, was gruff. "I've wanted to take you hard and fast since the moment you climbed down from the wagon that first day."

Matilda couldn't believe his words. She turned in his arms to face him, intent on seeing his face. "I thought you didn't like me. You said you didn't want a wife."

The corner of his mouth twitched until it curved into a half smile. "I didn't want a wife I'd have to spend the rest of my life holding back what lies deep within, worrying whether or not I'd hurt her every time we crawled between the sheets."

Dawson's hand wandered to her bare breast. He weighed it in his palm, rolling her turgid nipple between his thumb and finger until she gasped from the combined pain and pleasure.

"And when Duncan first showed me your picture, or should I say your sister's…" He quirked an eyebrow, carrying out the word until Matilda nodded in affirmation. Evidently Dawson received the answer he was looking for because he continued, "…picture, I was madder than hell. Not only didn't I want a wife or to be set up by some misbegotten matchmaker, but I sure the hell didn't want a skinny wife I'd break in two the first time I held her tight and thrust home."

His frank talk made Matilda's insides tingle. Just hearing it had the ability to make her feminine muscles quiver but she refused to give into the need. If she did so now, they might very well never finish their conversation.

"Then you're pleased with my body, with me?" Matilda thought he was but there was a tiny part of her that needed to hear the words.

Dawson's arms circled her, drawing her closer to his body. The width of his chest, covered in a fine smattering of dark hair, abraded her nipples. "Hell yes, I'm pleased with you and if your body," he punctuated the word by cupping her ass in his hands and squeezing, "was any more perfect, you might very well kill me. I have a hard time staying away from you now as it is."

"Then why hold back? You can obviously tell I won't break."

His hand traveled back up her spine to tangle itself in her hair. With a tug, he tilted her head for a searing kiss so slow and deep it left them both gasping for air. He tasted every recess of her mouth, plundering and taking and then insisted on more.

Dawson pulled away and stared deep into her eyes. "I guess it was habit, darlin'. Either that or I was afraid of scaring you away, hell I don't know. But now that I know, now that I know you can take what I offer and cry out my name for more, there'll be no going back."

With the agility of a man half his size, Dawson rolled Matilda onto her back, parting her knees and settling atop her. Matilda couldn't break the near trance his gaze held her in. His green eyes were flecked with gold, their pupils dilated in arousal. "I didn't think I'd ever find a woman I could love but love is exactly what I've found with you, Maddie."

Matilda blinked rapidly. She could feel her eyes well with tears. "I didn't know. I've been afraid to hope, afraid if you found out about my deception, you might realize what you could have had and no longer want me."

"And what deception might that be, baby?"

He really didn't seem to know what had held her in fear since her arrival to the Rocking C Ranch.

"Pretending to be my sister."

"Ahh, now I see. I've wondered why you left home. Duncan admitted to coercing you into coming here from Dodge City by threatening you with the law but I never thought it was still troubling you."

"So you've always known but chose not to say anything?" Matilda for the life of her couldn't figure out why he'd do such a thing.

"Yes, I knew and thanked my lucky stars daily. Now tell me how you ended up here instead of your sister."

Matilda spent the next few minutes explaining how she'd ended up taking Melinda's place. By the time she was finished, Dawson was staring even more intently at her.

"If I were your father, I'd paddle your ass until you couldn't sit comfortably for a week. Of course, I know you well enough to know a spanking probably wouldn't have stopped you." His chuckle warmed her heart.

"Does that mean my punishment is over?" She sure hoped not. There was something about being dominated by her larger-than-life husband that had Matilda forgetting all about her vie for independence, at least for now.

"From the look of the clothes left on the bed, you still have several days left." Dawson shifted his weight, lodging his length between her thighs.

Matilda lifted her legs, wrapping them around his hips, locking her ankles at the small of his back. "Come into me. Please."

Lowering his head, Dawson nipped her bottom lip. "Not yet." He continued to nip and lave, tracing the seam of her lips, until she was writhing beneath him, canting her hips at his in a rhythm sure to send her flying in no time.

Just when her insides began to spasm in pre-orgasmic bliss, Dawson pressed her into the mattress with all his weight, stopping her motions in the process.

"Dawson." The word came out as a whine if ever she'd heard one.

"Not until you tell me, Maddie. Let me hear you say the words."

Her body trembled, teetering on the edge of something so wonderful it would surely steal her breath. It took her lust-filled mind a few seconds to comprehend what he was saying. When she finally did, Matilda took his face in her hands, pulling him down until their lips melded.

"Your love amazes me and leaves me breathless. The sensation is even more overwhelming than the love I hold in my heart for you. Never did I believe it could be this way, this intense."

Dawson thrust his hands in the hair at her temples and spread the inky length across the pillow before using it to anchor her for his kiss.

"Will you love me now?"

His smile was a sensual promise. "Forever and always, baby."

The days following their declarations of love would forever remain among Dawson's fondest memories, with one day in particular standing out. Just as had happened every day following Matilda's first spanking, he insisted Jess fix a picnic lunch for the men to eat outside. After they left, Dawson took his luscious wife to the bedroom where he proceeded to mete out her promised punishment.

When she finally finished setting the last of his garments to rights, Dawson relented and took her the way he'd been lusting to do since the very first day, when he'd begun preparing her tight ass.

"Oh God! Please stop torturing me, Dawson." Matilda's words hissed out on a breathy exhale.

"You need to be prepared to take me, Maddie." The thought of sinking inch by rock hard inch into her vise-like heat made his heart pound with such vicious intensity against his ribs that Dawson actually felt lightheaded.

"If I were any more ready, I'd explode."

Praying for patience and the knowledge he wasn't pushing too hard, too fast, Dawson lifted Matilda to her knees. The soft mattress below her knees cushioned her for his thrust.

Glistening from the lubricating cream he'd used to prepare her, the tight pucker of her anal opening felt warm and pliant against the head of his cock. With the utmost of attention to her body's signals, Dawson entered her, stopping when the flared head of his cock was buried within her.

"Oh!" Matilda bucked back against him, burying his length deeper within her tight confines, stealing all his good intentions. With a hand centered between her shoulder blades, Dawson pressed her upper body until her cheek rested on the mattress, leaving her hips high, her ass wide open for his possession.

With the fingers of his other hand, Dawson plucked and rolled her ultra-sensitive clit, only pulling back when her anal muscles rippled around his cock, proving the closeness of her climax.

"More, Dawson. Please don't tease me anymore."

Her ragged plea was all he needed to hear. Lust and all-consuming love drove him forward and he buried himself deep within the tight confines of Matilda's ass in one swift stroke, stealing both their breath.

"Yes! Oh yes!" Her scream echoed off the walls as her sheath rippled around him in wave after wave of sensation.

Dawson continued to plunge home and retreat, watching as her body accepted him, all of him. The vision of her submission, trust and love as she knelt before him proved to be too much and before Dawson knew what hit him, he was emptying himself in her heat, filling her with his seed.

What followed later that night, after they'd cleaned up and rested, proved to be among the most sensual loving Dawson had ever experienced. While slow and soft, the encounter lacked none of the passion.

CR80

The weeks to follow were more of the same and yet, in many ways, different. Matilda sent word to her parents and sister of her marriage and in return was promised a visit as soon as possible.

She continued to try his patience at every turn and on many occasions earned the flat of his hand against her ass as a result. It didn't take long for Dawson to realize he'd created a monster. Things settled into a quiet rhythm of Matilda doing her best to learn her way around the ranch without getting herself or anyone else killed or injured in the process, and for once in his life, Dawson couldn't think of a thing he might be missing from his life.

The only thing, besides work and his wife, to even cross his mind these days was how he could get even and repay Duncan, all at the same time, for meddling in his life. Wicked thoughts of matchmaking filtered through his mind but as of yet, Dawson hadn't settled on any one idea.

With his mind on different plans for Duncan, Dawson nearly missed Matilda kneeling in the middle of their bedroom floor. Seeing her there, her head bent over whatever was in her hands had him immediately worried.

"What happened, baby? Are you hurt?" He was running his hands over her body before she managed to get a word out.

"I'm fine, Dawson, just boxing up my wedding dress."

Dawson eyed the large cedar box sitting on the floor. He recognized it as the box that sat snugly within her hope chest. "Why are you doing that?"

Matilda rolled her eyes at him as if he'd asked an addlebrained question even though she knew damned well he had no idea when it came to such things. She carefully wrapped the neatly folded gown in what appeared to be fine linens.

"I'm preserving it for our oldest daughter."

Her words took him completely by surprise. Never once had he given any thought to having children. Hell, he'd been happy to find a wife who could love him and accept him, all of him.

"You mean…" Dawson swallowed past the knot of tears forming in his throat.

Matilda looked into his eyes then smiled a watery, wobbly smile. "I think so," she whispered. "Are you happy?"

Dawson gave a whoop of joy as he collected Matilda against his chest, spilling them both to the floor in the process. He turned at the last minute so she landed on top. "Good Lord, woman. How could I not be happy?"

A father?

He was going to be a father!

Matilda levered herself off him. Her smile was beautifully bright. Her unshed tears made her eyes gleam like polished obsidian, their dark depths stealing his soul.

"I know it's silly but I wrote these letters. One for our oldest daughter, should we have one, and one for a son."

"You're not being silly, darlin'. You're seeing to our legacy."

Her smile widened as if she were glad he understood. "When I left home this dress signified vows I had yet to take. My mother insisted I have a proper dress to be properly wed and at first I scoffed. Now when I think about it," she rubbed her hand across the slight mound of her stomach, "I want the same for any daughters we might have."

Matilda scooted away to once again lean over the garment in question. After it was wrapped and placed securely in the box, she added the letters she had written before closing the top. "I may not have much to pass on other than my unconditional love, but if I have my way, our daughter will have my wedding dress, the same dress I wore the day we started our lives together."

Dawson smiled at the fierceness in her voice and sighed knowing his she-cat would soon turn into a mama bear taking care of her young at any cost. It was one of the many reasons he loved her and had no qualms telling her so.

Maggie Casper

To learn more about Maggie Casper, please visit www.maggiecasper.com. Send an email to Maggie at maggie@maggiecasper.com or join her Yahoo! group to join in the fun with other readers as well as Maggie! http://groups.yahoo.com/group/sultrysiren

Something Borrowed,
Something Blue

Lena Matthews

Dedication

To Maggie Casper and Liz Andrews because they always know exactly what to say at the precise time I need to hear it. For handholding, butt kicking, and unwavering friendship. I love you ladies.

Chapter One

"If you let me use your bathroom I will be your slave for life," promised the dark-haired man hopping up and down in the hallway.

Azure Kerr didn't know whether to be amused or alarmed. It wasn't every day a strange white man danced in front of her door, but this was Los Angeles, so she wasn't too surprised.

She had only been in L.A. for a little over two years, but the peculiarity of the city still sometimes intrigued and astonished her. That was probably one of the reasons she kept the door open and hadn't slammed it shut in the face of the stranger. He appealed to her, much like the city itself did.

"And you think I'm in need of a slave, why?" She kept her hand on the door, not willing to be taken in by his plea. He looked adorable and all, prancing about as he was, but no way was she going to let some strange long-haired hippie use her bathroom just because he promised to indenture himself to her.

"Because it's the Christian thing to do," he begged, twitching more. "Please, I'm harmless. You can ask Jessie. I'm a friend of hers but she's not answering the door."

"Well, I guess I can't ask Jessie then," Azure pointed out, not budging from her doorway. Not as if she would have if Jessie had been home. Her neighbor was a bit out there.

Although she and Jessie lived next door to each other, they weren't exactly Lucy and Ethel. It was hard for Azure—a professional black woman about to hit thirty—to find common ground with a barely-out-of-her-teens girl who changed her hair color as often as she changed her men. She had seen more men come out of Jessie's condo than she'd seen come out of the closet on Jerry Springer. Azure truly tried hard to be open-minded, but it was hard as hell to ignore the ho-like quality her neighbor possessed.

"If she were here, I wouldn't be asking either." Reaching in his back pocket, between jiggles, he pulled out his wallet and handed it to her. "My license, my social security card, and every credit card I own are in there. Feel free to call the law, Blockbuster Video, or my mother, whose number is on my contact in case of emergency card, while I pee. *Please!*"

Amusement won out, hands down. No self-respecting serial killer would have a contact in case of emergency card in his wallet, let alone his mother's name and number in there. He seemed more desperate than deranged.

Stepping back, Azure gestured for him to come in. "Down the hall and to your right," she called after the sprinting man.

The man shouted over his shoulder as he passed, "You're a goddess among mortals."

Azure shook her head in bemusement as she closed the door. If he ended up killing her it would be no more than she deserved. Walking back to the small kitchen, she stopped by the roll-away island where she had left the newspaper spread out over the top and waited.

The pastel yellow-painted kitchen was one of her favorite rooms in the condo. It was also equipped with sharp pointy objects and heavy heavable things she could use just in case she was wrong about hippy boy. He didn't necessarily look psychotic. A bit unkempt in his stained, frayed jeans and a metal-band T-shirt, but not crazy.

A loud groan filled the air, followed by the sound of water trickling. Azure winced as she wished, and not for the first time, for thicker walls. She was happy he had come to do what he said, but she really could have lived with less proof.

Even though he was doing exactly what he had beseeched entrance to do, Azure couldn't resist taking a peek inside of his wallet. Surprise, surprise— Mr. Gavin Connor of 650 Traveling Way, was one of the few people in the world who actually looked good in their driver's license photo.

He was really kind of cute, in a Seattle grunge band sort of way, with long brown hair teasing his shoulder blades and a killer smile. Tracing his photo with her finger, Azure reversed her thought. He was more than kind of cute. The boy was fine. Which only went to show it had been way too long since she had gotten any.

Her self-imposed celibacy reared its ugly head, reminding her once again she should be out getting some loving instead of boarded up like a spinster. It was pathetic actually, but her career as a wedding planner revolved around helping people bring their dream weddings to life, and yet Azure couldn't remember the last time she had went on a date herself. She was no closer to walking down the aisle for her own wedding than she was to sprouting wings and flying to the moon.

Yet at this point in her life, Azure would be happier to have a man pounding into her than proposing to her. Love and weddings were great and all, but sometimes a girl needed some good ol' fashioned sex.

The sound of the door opening and the echo of footsteps on the wooden floors alerted her to his presence. Azure closed his wallet quickly, not wanting him to spot her drooling over his license.

She was horny, not deranged.

"You, my love, are a life saver." Sticking out his hand, he introduced himself. "I'm Gavin Conner."

Azure looked down at his hand causing Gavin to chuckle in return. "Don't worry princess, I washed it."

"Shouldn't you be addressing me as 'Lord and Master' seeing as how I now own you?" Azure teased as she took his hand into hers.

His hand was callused, but the rough touch didn't turn Azure off, quite the opposite in fact. She was a blue-collar loving kind of girl. To her, there was nothing sexier than a man who worked with his hands—because if he knew how to use his hands out of the bedroom, there was no limit to what he could do inside.

"A hard task master it seems."

"Hey, it was your wager, who am I to look a gift horse in the mouth? By the way, your mother said to tell you to call home more often." Azure released his hand and held out his wallet to him.

Gavin froze in the middle of taking it from her. The look of surprise on his paling face was priceless, and Azure couldn't hold back her grin any longer. "Just kidding."

Shuddering, he pocketed his wallet. "You don't know how on the money that was. My mother is a bit needy."

"All mothers are."

"So are you going to introduce yourself or do I have to keep calling you 'Lord and Master'?"

The tone of his voice was flirty, surprising Azure a bit. Only a guy could be comfortable peeing in a stranger's home and hitting on her—all within a few minutes of each other. "I don't know if we're on a first name basis yet, slave boy."

"I know that you use Caress soap and like turtles. Doesn't that warrant me a name?"

"No. You peeing in my house warrants *me* a name, but not the other way around."

"I think you just like the way I say 'Lord and Master'."

"Could be." Azure looked him over as she picked up her coffee cup. He was so damn cute. She really needed to get laid. "So what do you play?"

Gavin smiled at her comment. "What makes you think I play an instrument?"

Repressing her grin, Azure thought he had to be joking. There was no doubt in her mind that Gavin was in a band. She might not listen to rock, but she did have to pass MTV to get to BET, and everything about him screamed garage band. From his shoulder-length, curly brown hair, to his tight jeans and rocker T-shirts, Gavin was born and bred for the lost generation. "Just a hunch."

"Well I don't."

"Really," she replied, eyeing his hair.

Following her thinking, he touched his curly locks. "I have an aversion to clippers."

Azure smiled, she couldn't stop herself. He was too much. "What?"

"Actually it's not just clippers. I can't abide any noise close to my ears. Can't wear headphones either." He winced as her grin grew larger. "Did I just lose cool points with you?"

"To be truthful, you didn't have many left after the prancing you did in the hall."

Gavin frowned. "I didn't prance."

"You practically did the first act of the Nutcracker."

"No pun intended, I'm sure."

"Of course not." She smiled. "So if you're not in a band, are you one…"

Azure stopped herself from saying "one of Jessie's many men". If he didn't know about the other men, then Azure would be putting all of Jessie's business in the street, and ho or no ho, Azure wasn't trying to blast anyone. "Are you and Jessie seeing each other?"

"No, she's the kid sister of one of my friends. He just moved away and I promised him I'd keep an eye on her."

Azure thought it would be rude to point out that so far he hadn't been doing a very good job of it. "How nice of you."

"I'm a nice guy." Gavin looked down at the open paper, and back up at her with a smile in his eyes. "So are you looking for a call out?"

If that was a line, he delivered it well. "Do I look like an actress to you?"

"I definitely think you have what it takes."

Although she had only lived in Hell A for a short time, she had already seen enough to know she would never make it in the biz—not that she wanted to. Azure relished her curves as much as she did her diversity and she was way too smart to fall for the "everyone has to be a size two" rule. Besides, she enjoyed her job as a wedding consultant to ever want to do anything else. "No, I love food way too much."

"It doesn't show."

"You haven't seen me without my clothes on." The silence followed by the slow smile spreading across his wide mouth made Azure want to kick her own ass for her comment. "Let's just pretend I didn't say that."

"You have as much of a chance of that happening as…"

"Me forgetting your little *demi-plié?*"

"I don't even know what that is." Gavin grimaced. "But I'm sure I didn't do that."

"If you say so."

"Anyone ever tell you you're a cruel woman?"

"I have a younger brother."

"Enough said."

"Well..." Azure started.

"So..." he said at the same time. They both paused and laughed.

"You can go." Azure gestured to the door with her hand. She didn't want to seem rude or anything but this was the weirdest conversation she'd ever engaged in with a complete stranger.

"I was just going to thank you for the use of your bathroom."

"You're welcome." There didn't seem to be much more to say. Azure hated awkward silences, so she headed back towards the front door, with Gavin traveling slowly behind her. Stopping at the door, she turned back to face him, jumping a bit when she noticed how close he was to her. Nervously, she wiped her palms on her trousers before opening the door. "I would say feel free to stop by again, but I doubt the situation will arise."

"I hope not." He grinned. "It was bad enough the first time."

"I think you handled it with decorum and grace."

Instead of leaving, Gavin moved closer to her and placed his hand a few inches from where hers lay on the door. "Are you really going to let me leave without telling me your name?"

"It's not necessary. Lord and Master will do just fine."

"Let's say for the sake of argument, I want to send you a thank you gift. A roll of Charmin or what not. Who would I address it to?"

"Did you flush?"

"Yes."

"That's thanks enough."

"You're not going to make this easy for me are you?" he asked, letting go of the door.

"I let you in my house, shared my bathroom and soap with you, I think I've made it easy enough."

"You know," Gavin leaned against the doorframe, seeming every bit as intent on staying as she was on him leaving. "I could just ask Jessie."

"I doubt if she knows it."

"I think you're underestimating Jessie's nosiness and my persistence."

"No, I think I have your persistence pegged down."

"You're only prolonging the inevitable, and increasing my interest in the bargain."

"Then I guess my work here is done."

All right that cinched it. It had been way too long since she had been laid. Even she saw the mixed signals she was sending.

Gavin stared at her for a few seconds longer, before stepping out of the door. "I'll see you later."

"Only if we run into each other in the parking lot."

"Oh no, there will be a later." He smiled. "Trust me."

Azure couldn't believe him. He wasn't going to just go away, and something about that was okay with her. The slamming of a door interrupted their silent stare and they both turned to see Jessie hurrying up the sidewalk. The girl paused in mid-stride when she noticed Gavin standing in front of Azure.

"Gavin," Her eyes appeared as if they were about to bug out of her head, much to Azure's amusement.

"You're being paged," Azure replied quietly, bringing his gaze back to her. "It's been real."

"You're talking like it's over."

Azure raised a brow at his audacity. "It is."

"Far from it," he assured her, giving her a wink as he turned to walk towards Jessie.

Stepping back into her condo, Azure shook her head in wonderment. There was no doubt in her mind—if it was up to him, there would definitely be a next time.

Chapter Two

Twenty minutes before Gavin walked through the door of Something Borrowed, Something Blue he'd been convinced that he was the most clever man in the world. Now, sitting in the waiting room with a family pack of Charmin next to him, he felt like the biggest ass in the world.

It seemed like a good idea at the time, but now he wasn't so sure. Gavin tapped his nails on the plastic wrap as he looked around the posh room, impressed with what he saw.

Azure was doing well for herself. His angel of mercy obviously ran a tiptop business, if the cut of the furniture was anything to go by. The phones had been ringing off the hook since he sat down to wait for her, and the little drill sergeant behind the big marble desk had booked more appointments than he could count, all the while keeping a very astute eye on him.

The receptionist's chilly glare was enough to pucker his nipples, and not in a good way. Gavin didn't know if it was because he was trying to see Azure without an appointment or if it was the abundant package of toilet paper he brought with him that made her wary.

Gavin wasn't going to be intimidated, or persuaded, so easily. Especially after all the work he'd put in just to get her name from Jessie, who acted as if he'd asked for her first born instead of the name of her neighbor. She eventually gave it—begrudgingly—along with the little information she had on Azure, which equaled out to a tad more than diddly squat.

Lucky for him though, Azure, although a pretty name, wasn't very common, and with help from the Google god, he'd pulled up more than enough information to get him where he was today.

Hell, part of Gavin still wasn't sure what he was doing there. It wasn't like Azure was the most stunning woman he had ever seen, or the first black woman he'd been drawn to. All women were beautiful to him, and it wasn't a novelty or a new fad for him to ask a woman of a different race out. Gavin considered himself an equal opportunist. He'd never met a woman he didn't like, but there was just *something* about Azure.

And that something was why, after the many odd looks he'd been given, he was still waiting to see her again, if only for one more moment. This was insane, but before Gavin could talk himself into leaving, a distant sexy voice traveled down the hallway and into the room, the elegant speaker not far behind it. Gavin would have recognized her voice anywhere, Lord knew it had been playing on repeat in his mind every day since they'd met three days ago.

"Cybil, has there been any word from MacDonald about scheduling a viewing of Rossi's Garden?"

"No ma'am."

"Damn it. I need to get in there before they're all booked up."

Rossi's Garden! Azure was trying to get into there. Life had never been that easy for him before. Apparently the Lord really did take care of children and fools.

"I left another message, my fifth one this week, but I keep getting the same reply. They'll call as soon as they have an opening."

"I know. You're doing a great job." Azure sighed as she glanced down at her watch. "I'm going to head out to lunch now, call me on my cell if anything comes up."

"Something already has." Cybil gestured behind Azure to Gavin who'd stood as soon as she walked into the room. "This gentleman has been waiting to speak with you."

"Really." Azure turned to greet him, a professional smile on her full lips. Her eyes widened as if she recognized him, but it was the only clue Gavin received that she remembered him. Azure was going to try to keep it professional, he could tell. In her gray power suit, she might have pulled it off—if it wasn't for the twinkle in her dark brown eyes.

"Azure Kerr." Gavin took her hand in his, completely dismissing the distrustful receptionist from his mind. "Welcome to later."

Her full lips trembled with unsuppressed amusement. "Hello again." That was all she said, but it was enough. Her smooth, sophisticated voice did things to him that porn and *Playboy* never had.

Yesterday her sable hair had been down, hanging loose and swinging playfully around her chin when she talked, yet today she had it pulled back and twisted into a bun, bringing her full exotic features into view. The dark eyes he couldn't get out of his head last night now were framed behind a set of wire-framed glasses that probably cost more than his work boots. She was just as attractive in her work wear as she was in her casual clothes, and still making his heart speed up.

"I think he's a wholesaler."

Cybil's words drew Azure's gaze down to the toilet paper still sitting on the chair where he'd left it, instantly making Gavin feel like an idiot. The feeling didn't last long though, because the second her gaze, which was brimming with amusement, connected with his again, Gavin knew she not only got the joke, she appreciated it.

"You really didn't have to." Her voice, filled with laughter, washed away any remaining doubt he might have had. "Really."

"Oh, but I did." And he wasn't just talking about bringing the toilet paper. Gavin had felt an irrepressible urge to contact her again. He needed to see for himself if she really was as irresistible as he thought she was. Answer received. She was.

"How did you find me?"

"It wasn't hard." Well, not as hard as quantum physics. "Besides I told you I would."

"That you did." The silence of the room was overwhelming as it became more than obvious they'd attracted a crowd. "Let's slip into my office for a second."

Gavin was willing to slip into anything of hers. Grasping her present, Gavin followed her down the hallway. He tried without success, to keep his gaze from settling on the soft curve of her generous ass, but it was like telling his heart not to beat.

Thankful that he was walking behind her and not beside her, Gavin enjoyed the view and made a mental map of the quickest way to remove her skirt without wasting needless time or energy searching for the phantom zipper.

They reached her office way too soon for his personal enjoyment. Gavin could have spent several hours just staring at her ass. Ushering him in, Azure gestured for him to have a seat as she closed the door partially.

She stood for a moment by the entrance, as if still in shock by his presence. "I really don't know what to say. Wait, yes I do. How did you find me?"

"You asked me that already."

"You didn't answer." Azure made her way around the desk, distancing herself from him in the process.

"With a beautiful, unique name like Azure, did you really think it would be hard?" Trying to look as unimposing as possible, Gavin dropped the package of tissue on the ground next to his seat then sat casually down across from her, giving her the space she so obviously needed. "By the way, I love the connection with your name and the name of your business. It's classic."

"Thank you, I wish I could take all the credit for it, but it was my partner's idea."

"*She's* a clever lady." At least he hoped it was a she.

"Yes, she is." Azure smiled, obviously catching on to his attempt at fishing for more information. "I didn't know Jessie knew what I did for a living."

"She didn't but it wasn't hard to find out after she told me your name. We do live in the century with the internet superhighway, remember?"

"That we do." Azure shook her head, bemused. "I'm still reeling about you being here."

He was reeling that she hadn't called security. "I wanted to see you again and I thought this might be better than staking out your house."

"Well, I appreciate it, I think."

"Just think?"

"I'm still not too sure about you."

"I bet I could change your mind."

"Charm isn't everything."

She thought he was charming? That was a start. "I hear you're having a problem getting in to tour Rossi's. What would you say if I told you that I could get you in?"

"I'd say you're delusional as well as cute." Azure snorted. "I've been trying to get an appointment with them for the last two months, and that's just to view the grounds."

Charming and cute. Things were really looking good for him. "Wasn't impressed with the layout online?"

Eyes narrowing, Azure crossed her arms over her bountiful chest. "Why do you know so much about them?"

"I have connections."

"To what?"

"To people." Gavin grinned. "What did you think I meant?"

"I'm still not sure. You're an odd one."

"I'll take that as compliment."

"Can you really get me an appointment?"

The hint of distrust mixed with hope in her voice made him want to laugh. She was playing coy, but he had her attention. "Without a doubt."

"How?"

"Haven't you noticed how resourceful I am?"

"So far the only thing I've noticed is that you're a possible stalker."

Gavin couldn't fault her for thinking that. "Does that work for you?"

A faint smile played at the corner of her mouth. "Normally, no."

"Normally…"

Azure gave him a bemused look as she gestured towards the toilet paper. "I wouldn't exactly call this normal."

"What can I say? I like to make an impression."

"Consider me impressed. I'd be even more impressed and grateful if you got me in."

Now they were talking. "How grateful?"

"Cut the bull." Azure raised a brow haughtily. "What do you want?"

"I want you to have a drink with me."

"I don't think so." Azure shot his suggestion down as quickly as he had brought it up.

But Gavin had known she was going to say that. He just refused to be easily detoured. "A business drink," he countered. "At the Garden. Rossi's has a wine bar with an excellent menu."

"I don't know what kind of women you're used to, but I'm not the type to whore myself for my clients."

"I don't know what your idea of drinks are, but mine doesn't have anything to do with sex." Gavin was offended that Azure would think he was insinuating such a thing. "I just want to get to know you better."

Eyeing him warily, Azure studied him, much like she had when she first opened her front door. She didn't order him out of her office though, so that had to mean something.

"Seriously, no strings attached. You meet me at the Garden, I'll be on my best behavior—hell I'll even wear a tie." *If I can find one.* "It will be nice, civil and even though I'm buying, I'll give you the receipt and you can write it off on your taxes. Strictly on the up and up."

"Drinks and nothing more?"

"Drinks and nothing more," he parroted, mentally crossing his fingers. Gavin wasn't going to push her, but he wouldn't turn her down if she changed her mind either.

"Fine," Azure said, uncrossing her arms. "But if you get out of line, I won't have a problem with ramming my fist down your throat."

"Duly noted." Gavin fought hard to suppress his smile. She was a bloodthirsty little thing. "But just so you know, if you try to take advantage of me, I won't fight back too hard."

The twinkle was back. "Noted, but before we go any further," Azure leaned forward and pressed the speakerphone button on her phone. "Cybil, could you please connect me with Rossi's Garden's?"

"Yes, ma'am."

"Ye of little faith." Shaking his head, Gavin stood and walked over to the desk. "Don't you trust me?"

The phone buzzed as Cybil's voice came over the line. "The phone's ringing."

Azure pushed the phone towards him like a challenge. "Make the call and I will."

Tsking, Gavin turned the speaker towards him. "You're too young to be so cynical."

"Rossi's Garden. This is Rory speaking."

"Rory, this is Gavin, is my sister there?"

The look on Azure's face was priceless as she mouthed, "Sister?"

"Yes, Gavin, hold on." The second the music came on, Azure smacked him in the arm.

"You're rotten."

"What time should I pick you up?" Now all he had to do was find a tie.

Chapter Three

"It's just a business meeting," Azure mumbled for the hundredth time as she stood in front of her open closet wearing only a bra and panties.

"Then why are you having such a hard time finding something to wear?" questioned her best friend and business partner, Janae Ward. She was sitting on Azure's bed eating chips and flipping channels. Janae looked out of place on the floral comforter dressed in all black, her normal choice of clothes coloring.

As soon as word had gotten around that Gavin had left the premises, Azure had been bombarded with questions she really didn't have an answer for. And no one had been more persistent than Janae, who insisted on accompanying Azure back to her home while she got ready for her "not date".

"I have absolutely no idea." Turning around, she walked back to the bed and plopped down on it in despair. This was way harder than it should have been. Finally after months of trying, Azure was going to be able to tour the Gardens, possibly get on their list, and yet she wasn't as thrilled as she should have been. She was petrified. "I should just call and cancel."

"The hell you will." Janae dropped the remote on the bed in disgust. "Get your big butt in that closet and find something halfway ho'ish to wear."

"I'm not going to dress like a ho for a business meeting."

"Please, if this is a business meeting then these chips are fat free, and I said half-way ho'ish. Don't show him all the goods, just tease him."

"Why would I want to do that?"

"Because you've been talking about him for the last three days, and bam, he shows up. With toilet paper no less, just to see little ol' you. If that's not a reason to show a man some goods then I don't know any." Janae nudged Azure in the rear with her foot. "Besides, what's the big deal? You're acting like you've never been on a date before."

"It isn't a date." Okay, even she didn't believe that. It wasn't set up as a date, but she sure was acting like it was one. The butterflies in her stomach and her sweaty palms were a dead giveaway. Azure wasn't fooling herself any more than she was fooling Janae. "This is your company too, you know. Maybe you should go with me."

"Ehh no." Janae held her hand up, blocking Azure's words. "I'm not chaperoning two grown ass adults."

Rolling her eyes, Azure stood and made her way back to her closet, hoping against hope something would pop out this time. Inspiration struck as she pulled out a gray dress that she normally wore to church and spun around holding it up to her, to get Janae's reaction, which was a prompt snort. Exasperated with Janae and the situation at hand, Azure dropped the dress to the ground in a funk. "Fine then, you come pick something out."

"Fine, I will." Janae got off the bed and pushed Azure jokingly out of the way. In her normal bossy manner, Janae peered into the closet. In less than thirty seconds, she spun around with a black silk blouse in her hand. "Hey, isn't this mine?"

"I'm borrowing it."

"For three months?" Janae snorted as she turned back to the closet and began shuffling through the clothes.

"I'm still waiting on the perfect outfit to wear it with," Azure lied, knowing she had no intention of returning the pretty blouse.

"I've got it." Holding up a black, ankle-length skirt that had a thigh-high split up the side, and a red wrap-around blouse, Janae looked as if she had just struck oil. Seeing Azure's look of discontent, she sighed and leaned against the doorframe. "Girl, what is wrong with you?"

"I don't think this is a good idea." In fact, Azure knew it was a bad idea. This evening had very little to do with the Garden and more to do with spending more time with a man. Something she hadn't wanted to do in eons. For the last few years, life had been all about work for Azure, and Gavin, in the small time she'd known him, had her focusing on something else. Him.

"Why?"

"Because we shouldn't be mixing business with pleasure."

"So it is pleasure, huh?" The slow smile spreading across Janae's lips made Azure want to cringe. Of course she would pick up on that.

"You know what I'm saying."

"Look you're going, and you're going to have a good time. It's been ages since you went out on a date."

"Thanks, Mom," Azure said sarcastically as she snatched the outfit from Janae's hands.

"I'm just trying to be supportive, heifer."

"What's wrong with me? I'm acting like I'm twelve."

"Do you think it's the race thing?"

That wasn't it, not really. Azure had never gone on a date with someone of a different race, but only because the opportunity had never presented itself. "It's not the race thing. It's an 'I'm scared thing'. I would be this scared if his name was Jerome and he was as black as night, but at least then I'd know Jerome and I would have something to talk about."

"What makes you think you won't have something to talk about with Gavin?"

"Because when I look at him, talking isn't what I have on my mind."

"Well, go ahead then."

"No, because it's not a date," Azure declared again, as she pulled on her skirt, hoping if she said it enough times she would begin to believe it.

"Did you shave your legs?"

"Yes." Azure chuckled, as she righted her skirt.

"Hmm."

"What's that about?"

"You can fool yourself, but the razor never lies. Did you trim the coochie?"

"Shut up," Azure muttered, heat filling her face. She had made sure that everything was nice and neat when she was in the shower, hitting everything with the razor and spritzing on her perfume between her legs and the twins.

"Oh yeah," Janae's tone held the same hint of satisfaction that her smile did. "It's a date."

 ∞

It's not a date. It's not a date. Damn, he looks good, but it's still not a date. It was a mantra Azure couldn't stop replaying in her head. For a very good reason. The man looked great. There were no two ways around it. Gavin cleaned up good. In black slacks and a tight charcoal-gray pullover, he looked like he could be a model for Abercrombie & Fitch and not like a man in desperate need of a lavatory.

When she pulled up in front of Rossi's Gardens, Gavin was waiting outside for her, scoring points left and right with his manners and charm. Not that he had any strikes against him. Since the moment she'd met him, Azure had been taken in by his presence and today was no exception. But this was about business. Nothing more, nothing less.

Sure it was.

"I see you made it." Gavin held his hand out to her, helping her from her car.

"I've only driven by here a dozen times. I'm sure I could find this place in my sleep."

"My sister will be pleased to hear that."

"As well she should be." Azure hadn't even gotten inside and she was already impressed. "This place is amazing."

"Wait until you've seen more of it. There's a reception taking place in the west pavilion, and an engagement party in the Tea Garden, so we have to steer clear of them, but everything else is pretty much up for show."

"I can't wait."

"Words I love to hear from a beautiful woman. I have to say," he said, turning to her, "that I half expected you to back out."

"I've been dying to get inside of here for months."

"Is that the only reason?"

"Of course."

"Hmm." Gavin didn't sound like he believed her, which was a good thing since she'd lied, but Azure simply smiled in lieu of a reply. She was going to keep this as professional as possible, at least while they were at the Gardens.

They walked in comfortable silence through a picturesque white picket fence, which led them down a path, past a miniature white chapel and a cascading waterfall.

Pad in hand, Azure quickly jotted down notes, pausing several times to take pictures. Sighing contentedly, she took a moment to take everything in. Rossi's Gardens was everything she expected and more. With its manicured lush lawn and gardens surrounded by large oak trees and man-made ponds, it was destined to make some lucky bride a wonderful setting for her dream wedding.

"I'd say from your sigh, you approve."

"Approve?" Azure turned to him wide-eyed. "I love. This place is wonderful."

"Thank you," a female voice called out, startling Azure and eliciting a growl of discontent from Gavin. "I love it, too."

"What are you doing here?"

The disgruntled tone in Gavin's voice surprised Azure, but obviously not their visitor, who just smiled at him. "Last time I checked, I owned this place."

"I told you I'd show her around."

"So does that mean I'm not allowed to come over and introduce myself?"

"Yes."

"Too bad." The woman stuck her tongue out at Gavin before turning to Azure and offering her hand. "I'm Gail Rossi, this big bully's sister, and proud owner of Rossi's Gardens."

"I'm Azure Kerr, part owner of Something Borrowed, Something Blue, and I think you have every reason to be proud. This place is amazing."

"Amazing, huh?" Gail winked at Gavin. "I like her."

"So do I, now go away."

The sibling dueling made Azure want to laugh, and oddly made her miss her own brother, the bane of her childhood. Despite Gavin's blustering, there was a real sense of love in their banter, something only someone with siblings would see.

"Not just yet."

"Gail."

"Gavin," she growled back, just as menacing. "Why don't you offer our guest a drink and leave us to talk awhile?"

"About what?"

"Business of course. That is why you brought her."

"Not entirely." Fuming, Gavin turned back to Azure who was trying her best not to chuckle. "Would you like a glass of wine?"

"Shiraz, if you have it."

"We do." Gail flicked her fingers at Gavin. "Go away."

"I'll be back." Gavin looked from Gail to Azure and added, "As quickly as possible."

"I'll be fine."

"I think he's more worried I'll run you off."

Startled, Azure looked from Gavin's retreating back to Gail who eyed her speculatively. "Why would he think that?"

"Because he's paranoid."

It's not really paranoia if someone's out to get you, ran through Azure's head, but luckily not through her lips. This wasn't exactly how she pictured the evening going. "I don't think he has anything to worry about."

"Not easily scared?"

"I don't run."

Her comment seemed to please Gail. "That's what I like to hear. When he told me he was bringing you by, I have to say I almost had a heart attack. The first thing I did, of course, was to pull your site up on the computer and get as much information about you as I could."

"Why?"

"Because I wanted to meet the woman who made my brother smile again."

"Again." Azure's brows rose in confusion. "I don't recall not seeing a smile on his face."

"Really?"

"Honestly. He seems like to me one big ball of fun."

"He used to be, that's for sure." There was a far off lilt in Gail's voice, making Azure wonder if she even wanted to know what was going on.

"Look, I think you might have the wrong impression of what's going on here. Gavin getting me in to see the Gardens was a favor. Actually he was returning a favor, sort of."

"The bathroom thing, right? He's told me about it. Countless times."

"He has?"

"Yes." Gail smiled. "I'm not going to bombard you with questions or anything, I just wanted to see what all the fuss was about. Now I see."

Azure was glad someone saw, because she was confused as hell. "Okay."

Gavin quickly made his way back towards them.

"We've had a few cancellations recently. I'll email you the dates this evening, and you can let me know if any of your clients might be interested in them." Gail offered.

It was more than she'd ever dreamt for. In fact, it was almost too good to be true. "And in return?"

"In return nothing. Consider it my way of thanking you."

"For what?"

"For that." Gail gestured to Gavin who stopped next to them with a smile on his face. "Now, never let it be said I don't know when I'm not wanted."

Gavin snorted. "It's been said, now shoo."

"It was very nice to meet you, Azure. I look forward to seeing you again."

"I as well. Thank you for allowing us to take a tour."

"It was my pleasure." With that, Gail exited as quickly as she had joined them, leaving Azure more confused than ever.

Handing her a glass, Gavin gestured after his sister with a sheepish look on his face. "Sorry about that, my sister is a bit annoying."

"All sisters are, just ask my brother." They laughed politely before lapsing into a comfortable silence, content to just stand in one another's presence.

Soft music beckoned from afar, and without speaking, they began to walk towards a veranda where couples danced under the evening sky. Azure was happy just watching, but Gavin was of a different mind.

"Let's dance." It was more of an order than a request, but since it was on a par with Azure's own desires, she gladly gave in. Being held by Gavin was not a hardship, especially because they seemed to fit together as if made from the same mold.

They danced in silence for a few minutes. Both moving as if one to the same seductive beat. His chest felt like granite under her cheek, but the steady beat of his heart comforted her like nothing else had before.

Gavin brushed his chin against the top of her hair, nudging her gently as he asked, "Did she hook you up with any dates?"

Azure pulled back, pausing in mid-step. "You didn't ask her to, did you?"

"No, but I would have if she hadn't." Gavin pulled her back to him, picking up the beat as if she had never stepped away.

"Gavin." Azure sighed. "You really didn't have to go through all this trouble. Don't get me wrong, I really *really* appreciate it, but I don't want you to think you had to."

His chuckle resonated like a wave against her. "I don't do things because I have to, Azure. I do them because I want to."

"Do you always get what you want?"

"I sure as hell hope so, because I want you."

Chapter Four

From the looks of things, Azure was well and truly stunned by Gavin's statement. Not exactly the reaction he'd been hoping for. But hell, from the moment he pulled her into his arms, all he could think of was kissing her, touching her, making love to her.

Breathing in her sensual scent, Gavin tried his best to keep his hormones in check. "You look unbelievable, by the way."

"What, this old thing?" The teasing tone in her voice made him think there was more to that than she was saying. "You don't look so bad yourself, although I do notice the lack of a tie."

"Well, it wasn't so much the lack of tie, as much as it was the lack of a collared shirt to wear it with."

"You don't own a collared shirt?"

Gavin had the grace to look a bit embarrassed. He had hoped she wouldn't notice he wasn't wearing a tie. "Yeah, I was a bit surprised by that too."

"I'm staggered. You mean Metallica doesn't have their own business line yet?" Azure smiled.

"I'm surprised you know who Metallica is." Gavin spun her out, loving the way she laughed in surprise, before he pulled her back into his arms, where she so obviously belonged.

"Don't get too happy, I don't think I could name a song or anything."

When the dance ended, Azure made to pull out of his embrace, but was stopped short by Gavin's hand on the small of her back.

"No, not yet."

She seemed surprised and a bit amused by his actions. "We can't stay here and dance all night."

"Why not?" Gavin couldn't think of any place he'd rather be.

"Because I'm wearing heels and I have to work tomorrow."

Not good enough. "I'll make it worth your while."

"I don't doubt that at all." Azure stopped dancing and looked up at him regretfully. "Gavin..."

"I like the way you say my name."

"No," Azure whispered.

"To what?" Gavin asked, smiling.

"To everything you're saying and to everything you're not saying."

Instead of replying, Gavin chose to ask Azure a question which had intrigued him since the moment they met. "What made you let me in that day?"

"When I figure it out I'll let you know."

Gavin didn't say anything, instead he watched her, waiting for her to continue. To his utter regret Azure gave a little shrug, as if that was it. She looked as lost as he was on the matter.

"One more dance," Gavin insisted. Without waiting for her to reply, he pulled her into his arms, unwilling to believe this was it. The slow melody spun around them in a sensual haze as he caressed the small of her back, pulling her as close to him as the laws of decency would allow.

It wasn't enough. And the feel of her hardened nipples against his chest proved that it wasn't enough for her either. Gavin maneuvered them to a darkened corner, wanting just a few minutes away from the bright lights of reality. He didn't want to think about doing the right thing.

Which was a startling first for him. Gavin didn't think it was in him to want to feel something, anything for a woman again. Outside of having sex that is. But Azure was different. She'd been on his mind since day one, and despite his stirring erection, it wasn't just sexual interest. He was interested in knowing more about her.

"Azure?" He whispered her name like a question. A question that only she had the answer to.

Her sigh spoke volumes and the look she sent him, filled with desire and need, was all the answer he needed. The heat in her eyes was nothing compared to the fire burning inside of him. Time slowed and sexual tension floated between them like a thick billowy cloud of lust. A glass shattering behind them broke their eye contact but not the mood.

"I should be going."

Gavin wasn't a fool. Should be going was a far cry from wanting to go. Her confusion was written all over her face. The tell-tale signs were there. Azure wanted to stay, she wanted to be with him, but her own personal devils wouldn't let her take the next step.

He would never understand the way of women's minds. Even after his short marriage, Gavin was still as clueless when it came to women as he had been the day he first hit puberty. The one thing he did know though, was he couldn't make this decision for her. He could only let her know what he wanted and abide by any decision she made. No matter how much he disagreed.

"All right, I'll walk you to your car."

Azure nodded her head in agreement and turned to walk away, but was brought up short by Gavin's hand on her arm. She peered up at him, confusion marring her pretty brown eyes, until he slid his hand down her arm to take her hand into his.

Azure didn't comment, merely smiled. They walked hand in hand in blissful silence all the way to the parking lot, taking in the sights and scenes around them. The cool night breeze moved around them, filling his head with her stimulating scent. When they reached her car, Azure paused, seemingly at a loss for words.

Gavin released her hand, regretting it the instant he did. He knew the minute she got into her car and drove away he would never see her again. Her desire wasn't stronger than the walls she had barricaded around her heart, and if he didn't move fast, he would never get the chance again.

Gavin waited till she began to unlock her car, before he stepped up behind her. "Was the tour everything you expected?"

"Everything and more." Her words eased around his skin like silken fingers, caressing his feverish body, fanning his already over-inflamed desire.

"Are you happy?" he asked. Gavin moved his hand down her arm, and took the keys out of her limp hand.

"Yes, I think it will turn out great."

"I kept my end of the deal, didn't I?" Gavin turned her around so she faced him.

"What deal?" Azure's voice came out in a shaky whisper.

"Not to go over the line."

"Yes."

"The tour is over. There is no line." Pocketing her keys, Gavin stepped forward, moving her back against her car.

He could see from the look on her face that she was struggling to move past the attraction that had pulled at them from the moment they met. Being next to her all night, breathing in her enthralling aroma and not being able to make her his, was one of the hardest things he had ever had to do. If she wanted to go, he wouldn't stop her. But she wouldn't go without him having tasted her once.

"This is a mistake." Even as she protested, Azure moved her hands around his waist. Instead of pushing him away, or saying no, she wet her dry lips with her tongue.

Principles, pride, and morals all slipped away. There was no more fighting. Azure wanted him as much as he wanted her.

"I promise to be the best damn mistake you'll ever make," Gavin whispered, sealing his words with a kiss. A deep soul-searching kiss.

The first taste of her lips against his was electrifying. It was like Christmas, birthdays and the Spice Channel all rolled up into one. Pushing against her, Gavin nudged her lips open with his tongue, drinking in the first taste of her mouth. Her warm tongue slid over his as she accepted him into her, and he kissed her like he had wanted to do from the moment he first saw her.

Yet it wasn't enough. He wanted to feel more, to taste more.

Gavin moved his hands down her body until they came to rest on the gentle swell of her hips. Gripping her tightly, he picked her up, and made the few steps to the rear of her car, depositing her on the trunk, all without breaking away from her mouth.

Her mouth. The sweet, soft fullness of her lips was going to be the death of him. Never before had he been so lost in the gentle slope of a woman's lips. And he wasn't alone. Azure kissed him back, demandingly, as she urged him on, with soft mewing sounds and wandering hands.

The sexy skirt that had shown off her generous curves all night now gathered between her legs, lying like a guardian at her gate of paradise. He couldn't get close enough. Gavin slid his hand down the smooth satin of her skirt with one goal in mind. The material was no match for his overwhelming libido, and in seconds, he had it bunched up in his fist and halfway up her thighs.

With his goal in sight, Gavin moved between her thighs, and pressed the hard, hot heat of his bulge against her covered center. The only thing separating them now was the flimsy material of her skirt, their mutual underwear and a zipper, all easily fixable in his mind. One swift move was all it would take to sink inside her hot center.

He was seconds away from ridding them both of their clothing when a bark of laughter sounded out. Azure froze in his arms as reality came crashing down.

An animalistic growl tore from his throat as he jerked away from her tempting mouth. The gentlemen in him demanded he step away and allow them both time to compose themselves, but the savage Neanderthal lurking inside him insisted that he continue with what they both so obviously wanted.

Unable to separate himself entirely one way or the other, Gavin held her to him. His pounding heart in tune with her own. A need like nothing he had ever felt before bore into his soul urging him on.

"Azure." He lowered his mouth to her neck, his lips, his tongue, his breath, marking every inch of skin he could find. "I want…I need to taste, touch, feel every inch of you."

Her shaky laugh was nothing compared to her tattered pulse tattooing against his lips. He wasn't the only one who had been lost in the moment. It was impossible to reach the ripe age of thirty-three without realizing when a woman welcomed his touch.

She responded, she opened, she took him into her, all with a welcoming moan, yet still something held her back.

"You don't believe in wasting time do you?" she teased.

"No, I don't."

"You move at lightning speed."

Gavin pressed his hips forwards firmly against her. Azure's nails tightened ever so deliciously in his side as she groaned in pleasure.

"Tell me you don't want me, tell me that you don't want the same thing and I'll walk away." *Limp away slumped over would be more like it.* "Tell me that you don't want to finish what we've started."

"What you started."

"That you loved." As much as he wanted to bury his cock deep inside of her, Gavin pulled away, his body protesting with every step he took.

He needed room to breathe and she needed room to think. "We both know what I want. I think I have an inkling what you want, but I can't make the decision for you."

Azure slid down off the car, straightening her skirt with shaky hands in the process. A slight breeze blew through her hair, forcing the soft ebony strands to fly into her face. Gavin curled his hands into fists to resist reaching out and stroking her hair back into place. He knew if he touched her now, he would pull her back into his arms, and to hell with whoever walked by and saw. Just the thought of having her in the moonlight had him hard and aching.

Hell, who was he kidding? He'd been hard the moment he first held her in his arms.

"You know…" Azure gave a weak smile as she nervously brushed her hair behind her ear. "The right thing to do would be to shake your hand and call it an evening."

"Right for who? Better question, says who?"

"Right for me for starters. I just met you the other day."

Gavin tilted his head to the side and studied her. She was fighting hard to come up with a reason that this was wrong. Since he couldn't think of a single one, he wasn't going to be much help to her. "Does the lack of time really matter all that much to you?"

"It should." Azure smiled, answering him more completely than she probably realized.

"But it doesn't." It wasn't a question. It was a fact.

"This is going to sound cliché as hell, but I'm not the type to have a one-night stand."

"Who said anything about this being a one-night stand?" Gavin crossed his arms over his chest, doing everything in his power not to reach out and pull her into him.

"We just met…"

"I could probably break it down for you in hours and minutes how long ago we met, but it won't change how I feel, or how you feel. This is about you and me, Azure. The rest of the world be damned. Tell me what you want and worry about all that other shit another day. I want to be with you. I want to take you home and make love with you all night." Ignoring what he'd promised himself earlier, Gavin stepped forward and took her trembling hand in his. "What do you want?"

"I want you."

"Then that's all that matters."

Chapter Five

This was a mistake. Azure hardly knew Gavin. She was being irresponsible and so utterly not like herself that it was frightening. Then again, despite knowing all of that, she couldn't help the way her body reacted around him, or the way her heart responded to him. They had only met a few days ago, but intuitively, Azure knew this was going to be more than just a one-night stand.

That thought alone boosted her morale on the drive to her house, and propelled her to the front door when her nerves would have held her prisoner in her car.

Why the hell am I acting like this?

"Did you change the locks?"

Startled, Azure turned around and peered into Gavin's mocking eyes. She had been so lost in her own topsy-turvy thoughts that she hadn't heard him approach. "No, of course not."

"Then why haven't you unlocked the door?"

Azure looked down at her hand in surprise. She had the key firmly gripped yet she hadn't made a move to actually unlock the door. Only God knew how long she'd been standing there. Apparently long enough for Gavin to notice in any case.

"I was just getting around to that." Azure turned to unlock the door, but once again froze.

"So I see." Gavin stepped up behind her and took her hand in his, moving it the extra step necessary and slipped the key into the lock. Leaning forward, Gavin brushed her hair away from her neck, and whispered softly in her ear. "If you don't want to go any further, Azure, we don't have too."

He was giving her the perfect opportunity to just shake his hand and tell him it was a lovely evening. No more, no less. They could end it there and everything would be fine. Azure could continue in her safe little world, where no one frightened or intrigued her. She had principles damn it, even if her body disagreed with her. Yet the only thing her principles demanded was that she didn't allow herself to be just a one-night stand.

Shaking his hand off, Azure turned the key and pushed the door open. Azure stepped in the room, then quickly turned around and put her hand against his chest, preventing Gavin from coming in. "Before you take another step, I think there are a few things we need to get clear."

His lips twitched like he was trying to prevent himself from smiling. "Okay."

"I've never had a one-night stand before. That's not the type of person I am."

"I don't care about that, Azure."

"I do." It was important for Gavin to know that she didn't take her body or the giving of her body lightly. "This is an anomaly, but the one thing it won't be is a one time thing. If we make love tonight…"

"*When* we make love tonight."

"Fine." Now she was having a hard time not smiling. "*When* we make love tonight, it will be under the complete understanding that we both agree it has to happen at least once more."

"Tonight?"

"No. I mean, sure if you're capable, but I meant another night. We have to do it again. I refuse to be a one night stand."

"So far, I'm not finding anything about your rules I don't like. And Azure, I can assure you, I'm capable and willing to make love to you more than once tonight."

"Well…" Clearing her throat, Azure tried her best to get her raging hormones in check. *Damn, he's lethal.* "Condoms are a must. And if you don't have any…"

"I have plenty."

"Plenty." *Lethal isn't the word.*

"Yes, now unless you have anything to add, I'd like to make a few rules of my own."

Startled, Azure dropped her hand. It never occurred to her that he would want to have a say. "Of course."

"First rule is," Gavin stepped inside her house, forcing Azure to step back, "you have to come and come often."

"I think…I think that's acceptable."

"And my second rule."

This she couldn't wait to hear. "Yes."

Instead of answering her right away, Gavin took his time. He shut and locked the door, before turning back to her with a wicked gleam in his eyes. "I reserve the right to make up sexual rules as we go along."

"That's not exactly fair."

"What does fairness have to do with anything?" Stepping forward, Gavin closed the final distance between them, pulling Azure into his arms in the process.

His lips moved against hers, tenderly yet hungrily at the same time. The drive over and their brief interlude at the door seemed to have done little to curb his hunger for her, or vice versa. All it did was wet her appetite, and man, was she famished.

How they made it to her bedroom, Azure would never know. She was just thankful the condo had a simple layout, so it was easy to figure out. Because if it had been left up to her, they more than likely wouldn't have gotten past the front door.

Gavin edged her back towards the bed, never breaking their kiss in the process. His hands moved over her body as if she were already nude, cupping, caressing, familiarizing themselves with every inch of her form. Everywhere he touched he inflamed, until Azure thought she would combust from want alone.

Not one to be passive, Azure's hands roamed his body as well, but unlike Gavin, who touched her as if he had all night, Azure had a goal in mind. Getting him nude and inside of her in record time. Moving her hand between their tightly pressed bodies seemed almost a chore, but it was well worth it once she grasped the tail of his shirt in her hand and began to drag it up his rock hard frame.

She tore her mouth away from his and pushed him back so she could pull his shirt up and out of the way. Gavin laughed at her impatience, but made no move to stop her. In fact, they were of like minds.

No sooner had Azure removed his shirt, than Gavin returned the favor. Only he removed her skirt and underthings as well. In less than a minute, they were both nude and spread out on top of her bed.

His eyes heated with desire—desire for her and what she had to offer. It sent tremors through her body, as he settled at the apex of her thighs. The thick length of his cock brushed against her damp aching flesh, causing Azure to cry out with need.

A need that was echoed in Gavin's movements as he made his way down her body, leaving trails of kisses in his wake. He was as talented in bed with his tongue as he was out of it. Gavin didn't treat oral sex like a job, with a lick here or a swipe there. He took his time discovering everything she liked and disliked, teasing her and tasting her until Azure thought she would go mad from pleasure alone.

Wrapping her hand around the silk strands of his hair, Azure writhed beneath his talented tongue. It was too much, yet not enough—all at the same time.

"Yes…right there…" The words were as jumbled as the emotions sprouting forth. Never had anything hurt so good before.

Just when Azure thought she couldn't handle a second more, she came, crying out his name.

Her orgasm had barely subsided before Gavin disappeared to the end of the bed for a second, coming back with several condoms. Gavin tossed all but one of the condoms on the nightstand next to them

"Do you always carry that many around with you?"

Gavin eyed her as he ripped into the wrapper. "Do you really want to know the answer to that?"

Azure thought about it for a second. Did she really want to bring the ghost of past lovers into bed with them? The answer came as quickly as she had. Hell no. This wasn't about the past, it was about here and now. "No."

"Good, then I won't have to ask you why you have a scarf on your bed."

Following his teasing gaze, Azure looked at the white scarf, draped over one side of her headboard. If memory served, she'd thrown it there in the midst of her fashion emergency earlier this evening, but she wasn't going to let Gavin know that. "It's probably best you don't."

"For my sanity, I won't." Gavin settled between her spread legs, slipping one hand under her thigh and arching her body up for his. "Besides, I think we've done enough talking, don't you?"

Azure couldn't agree more. "More than enough."

She didn't want to talk. She just wanted to feel. Every solid, hard inch of him.

"Look at me," Gavin ordered as he placed the head of his cock at her moist center. "I want to watch you as I take you."

The feel of his cock, so close to sinking into her depths, had Azure arching up to him, her eyes instinctively closing. But Gavin wasn't having that. He pulled back until he was no longer touching her, forcing Azure to focus back on him.

"That's right, baby. Watch me."

Unable to do anything but what he commanded, Azure kept her eyes focused on him. It took everything inside her to stay locked in his gaze, especially when he pressed against her again.

But once again, Gavin surprised her. Instead of pushing his length completely inside of her, he pressed the head of his cock just within her before easing back out. He plunged forth once more, but as before, he held back from sinking fully inside her.

"God, you feel so good," Gavin growled as he pressed forward. He was performing a torturous tango. Keeping her on edge — primed, ready and aching for his full possession — but never quite giving her everything she needed.

Unable to stand his teasing lovemaking a second longer, Azure pushed her hips up, driving him fully into her deep warmth. The pleasure was so intense that she cried out his name. Everything around her faded away as she focused all of her energy on the all-consuming sensations he instilled inside her.

Gavin's rough chuckle danced across her neck like a whispering wave. "So impatient, love."

"Stop teasing me and fuck me."

"No." He accentuated his word with a deep thrust of his hips, which stole Azure's breath away. "We're not going to fuck, Azure. What we're going to do is make love."

"Then make love to me. Just stop torturing me." Fuck, screw, bang— Azure didn't care what he called it, as long as he did it.

"Loving you could never be torture."

"I'm going to kill you."

"If I don't die from this first." Gavin began to move slowly within her, ignoring her demands, letting Azure know, in no uncertain terms who was in charge.

"Please, please…" Azure begged. Digging her nails into his back, she took her frustration out on him the only way she could. She wanted to come, she wanted to come badly, but mostly, she wanted Gavin to power into her. To take her swiftly and as fully as she knew he could.

At this moment in time, romance was the last thing on her mind. She just wanted to be consumed by him.

"I love the sound of 'please' on your lips." Increasing his tempo, Gavin drove into her forcefully.

A low, frantic gasp tumbled from her lips, as she dug her fingers into his flesh and held on with all of her might.

"That's it baby. Take it. It's yours…I'm yours."

The exquisite pain of her desire was mind numbing. Never before had she wanted someone, or something, as completely as she wanted Gavin. If hearing "please" was what he liked, then "please" was what he would get. "Take me Gavin, please. Fuck me, fuck me, fuck me."

This time Gavin didn't take exception to her words, instead, he did just as she pleaded. He fucked her, over and over, pounding into her craving body, as Azure undulated beneath him. Her orgasm washed over her—not like a gentle wave, but like a tidal wave. It stole her breath. It robbed her of her strength. Her orgasm was so powerful it damn near vanquished her will to live.

Gavin wasn't far behind. Seconds after she moaned his name, he cried out hers, pumping his cock into her as he came. Gasping for air, Azure thanked the gods when he gently pulled out and dropped onto the bed instead of on top of her. Their combined weight, after that little work out, would have been the death of her.

Amused by the thought of death by sexual exhaustion, Azure smiled. This was one experience she'd never regret or forget no matter what the future held.

"Damn." Gavin muttered, running his hand through his disheveled hair. "That was…"

"Incredible," Azure offered.

"No, I was going to say good for the first time."

Cocky bastard. "Just good?"

"Just good." Gavin smiled. "I'm sure we can do much, much better than this."

"You think?" If he had the stamina, she had the willpower.

"No, baby." Rolling on his side to face her, Gavin cupped her check lovingly.

"I know."

Chapter Six

"See Rory? I told you. The boy is gone."

Startled out of his self-induced coma, Gavin glanced over his shoulder, surprised to see his sister and her assistant, Rory, standing in his doorway laughing. "What?" he asked.

His annoyance only seemed to spur the grinning duo on.

"You're right, Gail. He's a goner."

"I have no idea what you two pecking hens are clucking about and I really don't care." Gavin pushed back from the computer and stood.

It was obvious he wasn't going to get any work done. Especially now that his office had been invaded by Tweedledum and Tweedledee. It didn't appear as if he was going to enjoy any peace and quiet either. Working in a family-run business had its ups and down. Today was a down, because his sister seemed intent on busting his balls.

"We're talking about the stupid little face you've been making ever since you met a certain lady friend a few months ago." Gail centered her gaze on the tip of her nose, causing Rory to giggle.

No matter how infatuated he was with Azure—and he was—Gavin knew without a doubt he hadn't been walking around looking like the stupid face Gail was making.

And they said men were immature. "Grow up."

"I don't want to." Gail nudged him, eliciting a growl from Gavin. "Admit it, you have a *thing* for her."

"I don't have a *thing* for her." A *thing*, how stupid was that? "We've been seeing each other for a few months." Twelve weeks and four days exactly, not that he was keeping count or anything. "But it's nothing too serious. We just enjoy each other's company."

That was an understatement if there ever was one. Since the first night they'd made love, they'd been inseparable. Yet even if they'd been living together Gavin would have stuck to the same story. His love life, was just that, his. And even if he lost every last sense the good Lord gave him, he would still never, ever confide in his sister. She was like a revolving door. Anything she heard she spewed right back out.

"I don't know what all the fuss is about. I happen to think she's wonderful."

"Of course she is."

"And I think she'd make the perfect sister-in-law."

"Sister-in-law?" Rory chuckled. "He's only been seeing her for a minute."

"We're not getting married." Gavin's angry tone silenced all the laughter in the room.

Rory, shocked by his outburst, quickly tried to mend the situation. "Of course not. You've known her less than three months."

For Gavin, it had nothing to do with time, and Gail should have known better than to think that it would. "We could have been seeing each other for a millennium and my answer would still be the same. No marriage. Ever."

"Ever is a long time," Gail countered, her temper rising just as quickly as her brother's. "Are you really sure you mean that?"

"Did hell freeze over and I missed the announcement?"

"How long are you going to make all women pay for Trudy's sins?"

Now she'd gone too far. "You must have forgotten the rule, Gail. We don't talk about my ex-wife like we don't talk about the tail mom and dad had to have surgically removed when you were three."

"It wasn't a tail!" Gail bellowed, her face flushing in anger. "It was a growth."

"Right, a growth that resembled a bear's tail."

Gail looked from Rory's shocked expression to Gavin's angry one. "You are an asshole."

"And you're a busybody. Stay out of my love life, and I'll refrain from mentioning any more of our family's little secrets in front of your nearest and dearest."

Irritated, Gail crossed her arms over her chest. "You know what, you're completely right. I will stay out of your love life."

Finally, God was listening. "Thank you."

"You don't need my help anyway."

"That's what I've been trying to tell you," Gavin muttered. Now if Gail would only disappear as quickly as she had entered, his day might once again resemble some sort of normality.

Gail continued as if he hadn't spoken. "You can fuck it up all by yourself. And this time, when you let that stupid ex-wife of yours ruin the one good thing you've managed to find, I'm just going to sit back and laugh."

"Don't you have some picnic baskets to steal, Yogi?"

Gail swung with all of her might and slammed her fist into Gavin's stomach before storming out of the room. The little flash of pain was worth it, just to get her to leave.

Rory though, was still frozen in her spot.

Annoyed at her wide-eyed stare, Gavin asked, "Was there something you wanted to add?"

"No...I..." Rory glanced quickly over her shoulder. "Did she really have a tail?"

The day was looking up after all. "I have pictures to prove it."

"Oh." Her hand clapped over her mouth, quenching any further comment. With a smothered giggle, Rory followed Gail's retreat. To Gavin's relief she shut the door behind her.

If only he'd learn to lock it, or better yet, work from home.

"Mr. Connor, Ms. Kerr is on line two for you."

Better and better. "Thank you, Eryn."

Now this was what he really needed. "Hey, pretty lady."

"Hey yourself." The sound of her sexy drawl had him feeling better than he had in years.

"Did I call at a bad time?" Azure asked.

"There's no such thing with you."

"You're too much."

Gavin could practically hear her smiling through the phone.

"I need to ask you a big favor."

"As long as you know that it will come with strings attached."

"I'm counting on it."

"Then ask away."

"Can you meet me at Ballard's Antiques off of Oak and Miller? I just found the find of the century but I don't have a truck and they can't deliver until next Friday."

Gavin glanced down at his watch, then back at his desk covered in paperwork. He had a lot to do today, but nothing was more important than spending time with Azure. "I can. Can you give me a half hour?"

"That's not all I'll give you." She lowered her voice. "I'm all kinds of grateful, Mr. Connor. Can you ever think of a way for me to pay you back?"

Think, hell, blood was a requirement for thinking and all of his blood had rushed down to his cock at her simple turn of phrase. "I'm sure we can come up with something."

Azure laughed. "I'm sure we can. Wait till you see what I found."

"I'm hoping it's an eighteenth century sex toy."

"No such luck, pervert."

"Then what is it?"

"I've found my wedding dress."

CR&O

How the day had gone so quickly down the shitter, Gavin would never know. All he was sure of was that his sister wasn't talking to him and his girl had not only gone shopping for a wedding dress—he'd somehow become an accessory to it.

The worst part was Azure had looked so happy when he picked her up, and yet Gavin could barely fling a smile in her direction. He could tell his mood was taking a damper off her day, but he couldn't help dreading the argument that was surely going to come.

They had been having such a great time. Making love non-stop, spending countless hours together, just hanging out, and somehow Azure had taken it to mean more. Not that the time spent with her didn't mean the world to Gavin, it just didn't equal marriage to him.

With a heavy heart, he carried the trunk into her condo, feeling as if the heirloom case was weighed down by the weight of the world.

Azure, on the other hand, was off the wall with excitement. She had talked non-stop since he picked her up, which was a good thing since he had little to say.

"Just sit it here." Azure cleared off coffee table. "Thanks."

"No problem."

"So…" Rubbing her hands together like a child at Christmas, Azure looked from the trunk to Gavin's frowning face. "What should we do first? Look at my dress or talk about what's upsetting you?"

"I'm not upset."

Azure raised a brow. "Talk it is."

"Really, it's nothing."

"If this is any of that 'men are from Mars and women don't have a map there' bullshit, you're going to have to let me know, because I'm the type of person who's upfront at all times. I thought you were like that too."

"I am." Usually, Gavin added to himself. The last thing he wanted to do was argue with Azure, especially when he knew it was going to end badly. "I just have some issues."

"Who doesn't?" With a sigh, Azure uncrossed her arms and ran a hand through her hair. "I'm sorry if I inconvenienced you by asking you to pick me up today. You could have just said so. It wouldn't have been a big deal."

"It had nothing to do with picking up the trunk."

"Then what is it?"

"You bought a wedding dress." The words tumbled out before he could stop them, but instead of being upset by his statement, Azure looked amused.

"Scared you, huh?"

"Of course not." Terrified was a better word.

Azure shook her head in mirth. "Okay, this is entirely my bad. I guess any guy would be a bit freaked out if a girl he had only been seeing for awhile called him up and said, *'Hey, I bought a wedding dress.'*"

"You think."

"I was just so excited to finally find a dress like it." Excitement crept into her voice. "Do you want to see it?"

Hell no, was his first response, but he was able to keep it at bay. "Sure."

Gavin wasn't sure what he'd been expecting, but a plum velvet dress wasn't it. Looking up from the dark dress to Azure's shining face, Gavin wondered if he was missing something. *How in the world did she look at that dress and think wedding?*

Tired of waiting for his response, Azure shook the dress, causing the material to shimmy. "What do you think?"

Was it a trick question? "It's...purple."

Azure lowered the dress with a frown. "Nothing gets by you. Isn't it wonderful?"

"I don't claim to be an expert at this sort of thing, but aren't wedding dresses normally...white...and not so...confining?"

"This dress is late nineteenth century, so confining was something of a must and back in the day most wedding dresses weren't white. Women would wear their best dress when they married." Azure pressed the material to her body and spun around. "Isn't it just divine? I'm thinking of altering it."

"If you want it to fit I think you should. I think the previous owner was a bit...husky."

"I'm just going to keep talking like you never interrupted."

"Okay." He chuckled.

"I think I'm going to shorten the sleeves a bit and open up the neckline. I want to make it more modern but still keep some of the historic feel to it."

"You really know what you want."

"Of course I do." Azure rolled her eyes. "I'm a wedding planner remember. I do this stuff in my sleep."

"And marriage, that's something you want as well."

"Well yes, someday. Doesn't everybody?"

"I don't know about everybody. I can only speak for myself."

"Very true." As if sensing the seriousness of the impending conversation, Azure gently folded the dress, carefully wrapping it back up in the paper. "So speak for yourself—do you want to get married someday, Gavin?"

"No, Azure, I don't. Not again."

Azure nodded her head as if he had just asked her if she wanted one or two lumps of sugar in her tea. "Marriage isn't for everybody."

Surprised she was taking his announcement so well held Gavin rooted to his spot. "No, it isn't. You can love someone and want to be with someone and still choose not to marry."

"That's true." She smiled. Turning away, Azure placed the dress in the trunk, pausing to rub her hand lovingly across the material. When she stood back up, she walked over to him, and hugged him. "Thanks so much for picking me up. If I recall correctly, I have an IOU to deliver."

Shocked at her easy dismissal of marriage, Gavin pushed her back until he could look down into her upturned face. Could it truly be possible that she was willing to forgo marriage and just be with him? "Did you understand what I said, Azure?"

"Of course I did. You don't want to get married again." Azure reached for the hem of his shirt. "It was pretty clear. Now let's get to the loving."

Something felt off. "Work with me a bit here."

With a sigh, Azure stepped back. "Okay."

"You know I don't want to get married and you're perfectly fine with me?"

"Of course I am. Like you said, marriage isn't for everybody. I think it's commendable of you to be so upfront about it."

"I'm…amazed." That was putting it lightly.

"Why?"

"I didn't think you'd be willing to give it up."

Now Azure was the one with the confused look on her face. "Give what up?"

"The idea of getting married."

Startled, she stepped back. "Why would I give up on getting married?"

Did he step into the twilight zone? "You just said…"

"I just said marriage isn't for everyone, not that marriage wasn't for me. I have every intention of getting married someday, Gavin. All this means is it won't be to you."

Chapter Seven

"You say 'not to you' so cavalier."

The boy was mad. There were no two ways about it. "I think I'm a bit confused. Do you want me to be upset that you don't want to marry me?"

"Yes." After a second of hesitation, he added, "No."

Azure tossed her hands in the air in frustration. "Okay, now everything's cleared up."

"Don't go getting pissy with me. You're the one who wants to see other people," he fumed.

"I never said that."

"Then what are you saying?"

"I'm saying…" Pausing, Azure took a soothing breath, trying to find her chi. If she didn't calm down, she was going to bash Gavin's head in with her beautiful new trunk. "What I'm saying is, it's okay if you don't want to get married. I enjoy spending time with you. No, scratch that. I love spending time with you. These last three months have been three of the best months of my life, but I'm not going to put my dreams on hold, just because the idea of getting married scares you."

"It doesn't scare me."

"Right." Azure drew out the word, putting all of her disbelief and amusement in it. "What I don't understand is, why are we fighting? I'm not the clinging type. If you say you don't want to get married, I say okay. I didn't go into this relationship looking to get married anyway."

Instead of her words easing the tension between them, it only seemed to add more. "Then what were you expecting?"

"To have fun with you. Enjoy the time we've been blessed with."

"So I'm just someone for you get a few kicks with?"

"Are you being daft on purpose?" This wasn't exactly the way Azure had pictured the day going.

Truth be told, when she'd first spotted the gown, she'd envisioned herself walking down the aisle towards a smiling Gavin. He'd played guest star in all of her fantasies of late, but his words dashed away any hope of her dreams coming true.

His attitude, although disappointing, wasn't surprising. Azure had pretty much figured out that he'd either come out of a really bad break-up or marriage just from what she'd learned from Gail. She'd never asked him point blank. She figured if he wanted her to know, he'd offer, but now Azure realized she'd been mistaken. Maybe if they had talked about his little phobia beforehand, they wouldn't be in this position now.

"No, I'm not." With an animalistic growl, Gavin ran his hand through his hair as if in frustration. "I don't like the idea of you marrying someone else."

Finally, something they could agree on. "But you don't want to marry me yourself?"

Sighing, Gavin slumped down on the couch like a perturbed child. His disgruntled expression was amusing and adorable all at the same time. Unable to ignore his pouty appeal, Azure walked to him and climbed on his lap, with her knees on either side of him so she could face him.

Gavin encircled her hips with his hands, securing Azure to him. "It's not that I don't want to marry you."

"It's not?"

"No. Hell, if I were ever to marry again, it would be to you, but I just don't see myself wanting to do that. Ever."

Although his words broke her heart, Azure refused to allow him to see it. "I don't know what happened in your past relationship, Gavin, but it has nothing to do with us."

His snort showed his disbelief. "The relationship wasn't the bad part, Azure. It wasn't great by any means, but it was better than the divorce."

"Was it ugly?"

"Ugly isn't even the word for it. The only thing I'm grateful for was we didn't have kids. I mean she fought me for a blender she never used."

"Not all marriages end in divorcee."

"But the majority of them do."

Azure wanted to roll her eyes at his pessimism. Yes, marriages failed. Yes, the success rate was lower than the failure rate. Still, when it was right— like it so obviously was with them, percentages didn't matter. When it came down to it, Azure was willing to risk it all for a chance at forever. Unfortunately, Gavin couldn't say the same.

"If it makes you feel better, I have my own blender."

Her attempt at humor didn't fall on deaf ears. "That does ease the pain a bit. The way I see it, we're at an impasse. You know what you want and I know what I want. The only question is, is there a middle ground?"

In a situation like this, Azure didn't see how there could be. "I don't really think there's a middle ground on something like this."

"We could move in together."

Azure eased off his lap, needing to put a little space between them. Moving in together wasn't a compromise. They would be no closer to being married than they were now. While she was fine with the state of their relationship now, Azure really couldn't see herself moving in with Gavin, knowing it would never go farther. "I don't think that's such a good idea."

"Why not?"

"Because there isn't really a point to it." Azure shrugged her shoulders.

"The point would be for us to be together."

"We're together now. Besides we've only known each other for three months."

"But if I proposed to you, the three months wouldn't matter." The anger in Gavin's eyes was nothing compared to the ire growing deep inside of Azure.

"This is not a competition. There is no right or wrong answer here."

"Sure there is." Gavin snorted. "It wouldn't be too soon for us to get engaged but it's too soon for us to move in with each other."

"All of this because I needed help bringing home a trunk?"

"No, all of this because you're not willing to compromise."

"And how are you willing to compromise, Gavin? Moving in together—which I'd like to point out we've never discussed before today—will get you ass twenty-four-seven, but gives you enough space where you don't feel suffocated. What exactly is in it for me?"

"I guess I'm not enough."

"I could ask you the same thing." Azure stood, and moved away from the couch, putting as much distance between them as she could without leaving her condo. "I'm not your ex-wife, I'm not any screwed up girlfriend from your past. I'm just me and I won't let you judge me by other women's mistakes."

"This argument is the mistake," he argued, standing as well. "I don't want to fight with you. I just…"

"Just what…"

"I just don't want to lose you."

Damn him, just when she was getting all worked up, he had to go say something semi-nice. Asshole. "I really don't know what to say to make you feel better and Lord knows I don't want to fight either, especially about something as pointless as this."

"I don't consider you seeing other men pointless."

"I never said anything about seeing other men."

"But you will. One day, you're just going to get tired of waiting around for something that's not inside of me."

"Or one day, you'll realize that it is. Either way Gavin, I live for today, not for tomorrow. And today, we have something that's really, really good. I'm happy with the way things are."

"But for how long?"

Gazing up into his soulful eyes, so full of hurt and confusion, made Azure want to do nothing more than to kiss his pain away.

Gavin was at a crossroads, and there wasn't anything she could do but love him and wait for him to realize just how much he loved her back.

"For as long as it takes."

CB&O

There was a lot to be said about a man who didn't take no for an answer. Azure couldn't help smiling as she signed for her third delivery of flowers this week. Although she was a lily girl, a dozen long stemmed roses had a way of getting a girl's attention.

But it wasn't just the flowers—it was the candy she dare not eat, and the cute stuffed frog she couldn't stop caressing. Gavin was acting like a man on a mission, and damn him, it was working. If he wasn't bowling her over with romantic gestures, he was making himself at home in her place. Every day, a few more of his things would appear, finding themselves at home amongst her things.

Ever since their talk, Gavin had gone out of his way to make himself indispensable to Azure. He was doing everything in his power to make sure she knew how wonderful things could be, if they only lived together.

Pulling out the card, she stared long and hard at the simple message inked out across it. *Everyday like today.*

It was a hard message to ignore, just like the previous ones had been. One thing was for certain, even though she wasn't going to give in to what he wanted, she had surely given in to the man himself.

Finding an empty vase proved to be an impossible task, so Azure took her time cutting the roses short and filling a clear bowl with water before laying the buds on top. Setting her new centerpiece on her coffee table, Azure moved towards her newest obsession, her trunk.

The cedar trunk was nowhere near as old as the dress itself, but still it was just as beautiful. The workmanship told of obvious handmade master craftsmanship and a sense of pride that just wasn't as evident in today's machine-made products. The real find, of course, was the dress.

Azure inhaled deeply as she opened the trunk. She knew it was odd, but there was just something about the stale air, the smell of the old leather and cloth she adored. This was actually only the second time since she'd bought the dress she'd opened the trunk, for fear of sun damage to her find, but today was special. Her dress form had finally come in, and Azure couldn't wait to see the dress the way it was meant to be seen.

Whoever owned the dress before she did obviously cared for it very well. Not only was it encased in the trunk, it had also been wrapped in acid-free tissue and placed inside an acid-free box to preserve its quality as much as possible.

Azure closed her blinds so direct sunlight wouldn't fall on the dress and possibly fade it, even though she knew it was a bit silly. She had bought it to wear, but still, she wanted to baby it as much as possible.

Shaking her head, she laughed at herself. "It's just a dress."

The words echoed around the empty room, making her feel even crazier than before. Not only was she babying the dress, she was talking to herself.

After unwrapping the dress, Azure placed it on the form, smoothing lines and creases as she went. The sight of the dress, filled out as it should be, actually brought tears to her eyes.

It was all Johanna Lindsey's fault. If she had never fallen in love with Lindsey's books in the eight grade, Azure would have never become obsessed with history and historical clothing and she wouldn't be in this position now, crying over an aging dress.

While other brides yearned for Vera Wang, Azure salivated over a one-piece princess-line gown in silk taffeta with a fitted bodice. Probably made by someone's mother. Still…it was perfect, and the wedding dress of her dreams.

With a smile, Azure went back to the trunk and rewrapped the paper and placed it into the box. When she went to place the box back inside, a rip in the fabric of the trunk caught her eye.

"Doggone it," she muttered, leaning forward to see if she could possibly fix the rip. When she ran her hand over the tear, Azure was surprised to find the side bulkier than it should have been.

How in the world did I miss that?

Carefully tearing the fabric a bit more, Azure reached inside, letting out a cry of surprise when she felt something. With a furrowed brow, Azure gently pulled out the wrapped bundle.

The package was covered in yellowed parchment, tied with red twine. Sitting down on the floor, Azure carefully untied the package and pulled the paper back. To her amazement a dozen or more letters spilled forth.

Azure opened the first one and what she saw took her breath away.

Chapter Eight

Gavin was a bit freaked out and the strangest part was he knew he really didn't have a reason to be. Azure hadn't seemed too upset about him not wanting to get married. In fact, she didn't appear to be bothered at all, which was why Gavin was disturbed.

Shouldn't she be upset? If she cared, really cared about him and a future with him, shouldn't she be bothered by the fact that he didn't want to get married? A better question though, was why the hell was he so upset?

Things weren't settled, not by a long shot. Gavin wanted a more permanent relationship with Azure. He wanted to move in with her, or hell, she could move in with him. What mattered most was they would be together, and together for Gavin meant living together exclusively, and more importantly, loving one another.

He already knew he loved her. Lord knew he tried to show her in a million different ways, yet he hadn't quite said the words, and growing up in a houseful of women, he knew words were important. So today, he was going to tell her. Just let her know he cared for her and loved her more than he had or thought he could love anyone.

Hopefully the words would be enough to close the door on any doubt she might have about his commitment to her.

Besides, who needs a ring? It wasn't that important in the long run.

As Gavin headed up the walkway to Azure's door, he instantly thought back to the very first time he came here. It would be a heck of a story to pass on to their grandkids one day, how Grandpa badgered Grandma into letting him come in to use the bathroom.

Smiling at the thought, Gavin knocked twice on her door, as had become his manner before unlocking it with his newly acquired key, and pushing the door open. The sight that greeted him had his thoughts turning from grandchildren to murder in a blink of an eye.

Azure, his woman, was in the arms of another man. A man who Gavin didn't know. Not that knowing him would have made a world of difference, because Gavin didn't like it.

The part bothering him the most, wasn't that in another life he would have thought they looked great together, both born from the same lovely dark clay of the earth, or the fact the man was clearly smitten with Azure. It was the way she was looking at him. Like he'd hung the moon. Selfish as it was, Gavin wanted Azure to look at him like that, and him alone.

Clearing his throat, Gavin pushed the door open. Surprisingly though, Azure didn't jump away from the man, instead, she looked over her shoulder, and smiled at Gavin.

"Honey, you won't believe what happened."

Gavin might be in the dark about what had her looking so happy, but he had a good idea what would make him smile, and that was ramming his fist down that grinning bastard's throat. To make matters worse, the son of a bitch still hadn't let her go. Suddenly a light dawned bright and clear. Here was a very good reason for a ring. It was the perfect calling card to warn men off. Maybe Gavin would have to rethink his position after all.

"What's going on?" *And get the hell out of his arms.*

Azure pulled away, finally, from the man's arms and rushed over to Gavin's side. "You won't believe what happened."

"First, who's this?"

"Good Lord, forgive my manners." Azure moved to go back to the other man, but was stopped by Gavin's hand on her arm. She sent him a quizzical glance before continuing, "This is Terrell Ballard, of Ballard's Antiques. Terrell, this is…"

"Gavin Connor, her *boyfriend*." *And the man who will kill you if you ever touch her again.* "Pleased to meet you."

The word "boyfriend" caused Terrell's smile to fall. Apparently he hadn't known that Azure was dating someone or that the someone was of a different race. From the way he glanced between Azure and Gavin, he wasn't too pleased by the knowledge.

Terrell recovered immediately though, but not quick enough that Gavin missed the distasteful look Terrell sent his way. It was enough to make him feel marginally better. At least he wasn't the only one unhappy with the situation taking place.

"The pleasure's mine." Terrell begrudgingly offered his hand to Gavin, who just nodded, much to Azure's displeasure.

"Anyway." Shooting Gavin a "behave yourself" look, Azure pulled out of his grasp and walked to the coffee table. She picked up a pile of papers and handed them to Gavin with a pleased look on her face. "Last night I found these in the wedding dress trunk. They're letters written from the original owner of the wedding dress to her heirs and then to their heirs and so on and so on.

The very first two were from Matilda Chandler in 1878. She wrote two letters to her unborn child, one in case she had a daughter and one in case she had a son. Her letters are basically about her life with their father and her take on love and everything in between. She wanted her wedding dress to be passed down in the family."

Azure's eyes filled with wonder as she spoke and Gavin couldn't help but become caught up in her tale. "The next set of letters were written by her daughter, Maria Chandler Schurman, to her daughter, Mae, who later wrote one to her granddaughter, Madeline."

It was almost too much for Gavin to take in. A whole family legacy passed on through something as trivial as a purple dress, but he could tell Azure was looking for him to say something. "That's a lot of M's."

"Yes it is." She laughed, clearly happy. "I guess it was another tradition passed on, because everyone who wrote a letter or received a letter, their first name began with M."

"And you were so happy you just had to call Terry, here…"

"Terrell."

"Whatever." Gavin shrugged the man's correction off. "To tell him of your find."

"That and to get his help."

"With…"

"Terrell is a genealogy freak like I am."

There was no doubt in Gavin's mind that Terrell was a freak, but it still didn't explain dick.

"And he's helping trace the dress back to the original owners. The history of this dress is just so…" Azure inhaled deeply as if trying to take it all in, "…vast, that I want to be able to pass the story down to our…I mean my kids."

"Our" sounded a lot better to him, and the fact it made old Terry frown was a plus as well. "That's wonderful, honey."

"Isn't it?"

"Yes." Gavin leaned down and brushed a kiss across her brow. "I think this is wonderful, and if I can help in any way…"

"I assure you, I've got it covered," Terrell interrupted. "I have all the resources I need to get Azure anything she needs."

It was on the tip of Gavin's tongue to remind the asshole that Gavin took care of all of Azure's needs. "My offer still stands," Gavin reiterated.

"And it's very much appreciated." Azure stood on her tiptoes and pressed a soft kiss on Gavin's lips. Not willing to let her go so easily, Gavin pulled her into his embrace and turned the thank you kiss into something a lot deeper.

Erasing everything from his mind but Azure, Gavin focused on the feel of her against him. The taste of her full lips, the gentle sway of her tongue against his. Everything about this woman worked for him. From her scent, to her flavor, to her heart. Azure was special in every way, and she was all his.

How long he held her in his arms, tasting her, drinking in the glory of her lips, Gavin didn't know, nor did he care.

This time it was Terrell who cleared his throat to get attention. Pulling back, Azure blushed as she ran her fingers through her hair. "Forgive me, Terrell."

"No forgiveness necessary. I've left Dawn at the store much longer than I intended, so I must be on my way."

Azure walked him to the door. "You'll let me know when you hear anything, right?"

"First thing." Terrell glanced over his shoulder towards Gavin, who was leaning against Azure's desk. "It was nice to meet you."

Somehow Gavin didn't quite believe him and since he didn't believe in lying, he didn't return Terrell's sentiment. "Bye."

"I'm just going to walk him to his car, then I'll be back." There was a bit of warning in her tone that made Gavin smile. Azure was so cute when she got riled.

Gavin sat on the couch and thumbed through the letters as he waited for Azure to return. Even he, cynic that he was, had to admit the letters and everything they represented was kind of cool.

"You weren't very nice to him." The words rang out just as loudly as the slamming door did. Azure stormed over to him, hand on hip, eyes narrowed in annoyance. *God I love this woman.*

"Was I supposed to be?" Gavin leaned forward and placed the letters on the coffee table. He wanted his hands free to deal with more important issues. "Besides, he wants you."

Azure rolled her eyes. "No he doesn't."

"Trust me, he does."

"Whether he likes me or not, the important thing is that I don't like him." Obviously irritated, Azure crossed her arms. "For the record, I'm not sure if I like you all that much right now."

"Yes, you do."

"I wouldn't count on it."

"I like you enough for the both of us." He teased, reaching out and dragging her to his lap.

"You're a big..."

"Speaking of big." Gavin pressed her down on his lap, making sure she felt every inch of his rising cock. "I like it when you get all feisty on me."

Azure's lips quivered as she tried to suppress a smile. "You're deranged."

"He was touching you. It's a caveman thing."

"Caveman, now that's a word for it." Azure turned and faced him, eyebrow raised. She looked so cute when she did that.

"Sit up, baby." Gavin eased her skirt up over her hips so she could straddle him easier. "Now isn't that better?"

"Better for who?"

"Better for me, and soon, better for you. First thing we have to do is get you out of this shirt."

"We do, do we?"

"You just sit back, and let me do all the work." With a patience Gavin didn't know he possessed, he slowly unbuttoned her beige blouse, loving how her breasts came into view, one button at a time. Her full brown mounds seemed to practically burst from their fawn, laced covering.

"You should be illegal."

"In some states I am," she teased, slipping her shirt off her shoulders.

"I can see why." Leaning forward, Gavin brushed his lips against the gentle swell of her breasts.

Gavin felt her nipple harden beneath his cupped hand, and leaned down to take the taut bud into his mouth, bra and all. Azure tangled her hands in his hair, pushing him harder on her breast. Gavin knew how much Azure loved having her nipples teased, almost as much as he enjoyed teasing them.

Moaning, she rocked her pelvis down on him, rubbing her hot center across his straining erection.

Gavin pulled back. "Did I say you could move?"

"You didn't say I couldn't."

"Then let me make it more clear." Gavin pushed Azure back a little so he could reach his pants buckle. After unbuckling his belt, he pulled it through the loops with one hand while grasping her wrist with the other. "Now be a good girl and hold still."

"Your wish is my command," Azure's voice lowered huskily as he bound her hands behind her back with the belt. The position made her breasts thrust forwarded invitingly, and beg for his touch. Gavin couldn't resist pulling them out of their lacy confines.

Azure was glorious. In all his life, Gavin had never encountered a woman who could make him hard with a smile. Her full lips instantly had him thinking of where he wanted her to kiss him next. The smooth, long brown legs of hers were made to adorn his hips, and her breasts—her breasts were what sonnets were written about.

There was one thing Gavin forgot to do when he unbuckled his belt, and that was free his straining erection. "Up on your knees, baby."

Azure quickly obeyed, rising from his lap to kneel above him. Her new position gave Gavin all the room he needed to not only retrieve his wallet from his back pocket for the rubber, but also to take his cock out of its tight confinement.

"I still think you have too many clothes on." Gavin gripped her thong in his hands, and ripped it clean off her body. "Now that's better."

Gavin couldn't resist getting a taste of her sweet nectar. Dropping her thong, he reached between her legs and teased her damp folds. When his fingers were saturated with her essence, he brought his hand to his mouth so he could savor the flavor of her. It was an action that bore repeating.

Azure trembled above him. "Gavin…don't tease me. Fuck me, please."

Gavin reluctantly pulled his hand away from her tempting treasure, missing the feel of her instantly.

After slipping on a condom, Gavin placed one hand on his cock to guide it into her heated center and placed the other hand on her hip, steering her down onto his waiting cock. "Ease down, baby."

The head of his cock slid into her hot depths, as Azure slowly sank down on his length, inch by inch. By the time she was fully seated, they both were a bit breathless.

Gripping her hips in his hands, Gavin urged her up, then down again.

"I can't…I need help…" Azure moaned as she rocked her hips forward.

"I'll set the rhythm, baby," Gavin gritted out. "You just brace yourself."

Holding on to her hips, he held them slightly up as he powered in and out of her wet pussy. With every thrust Azure moaned louder, rocking her body into his. This was supposed to be a position where Gavin had all the power, but he was powerless underneath her. Powerless to stop his hips from slamming up against hers and powerless to stop her pussy from milking him dry with every down stroke.

"Fuck, fuck baby."

"Gavin…Gavin…" His name was like a loving echo on her lips, urging him on, begging him for more. "I'm going to…so…close…"

"That's right, baby." Gavin sped up, pushing into her as hard and fast as he could. "Come for me, Azure, come for me."

Her body shook from the force of her release. Azure cried out his name as she came, her pussy quaking around his thrusting cock. It only took the first signs of her orgasm to trigger his own. Gavin gripped her hips as he erupted inside of her.

"Oh my...oh..." When words failed her, Azure buried her face in his neck and began to giggle.

"Are you laughing?" Gavin smacked her firmly on her ass. "Woman, don't you know you're never supposed to laugh at a man at a delicate time like this?"

Azure eased back to look him in the eyes. Her own were filled with laughter, her smile full of joy. "Delicate? You? Hardly."

"Stranger thing have been known to happen."

"Stranger than us?"

"Baby, this isn't strange," Gavin released her hands, massaging her wrists gently as he continued, "This is love."

Chapter Nine

Azure eased down in front of the trunk. She knew what she had to do, just as she knew she didn't want to do it. Opening the lid, she carefully inserted the letters back into the gap from which she had taken them.

It had only taken one phone call to bring her dreams crashing down around her. Tears flowed down her cheeks as she prepared the dress box. This was a lot harder than she thought it was going to be, that was for sure.

Even though she'd only owned the trunk and all the precious cargo it had brought with it for a short while, Azure still felt as if she was saying good-bye to dear old friend.

She was doing the right thing, though, because only the right thing would hurt this badly.

A swift knock on her door was the only warning she had before Gavin came strolling into her condo. His smile instantly melted away as he took in her disheveled appearance.

In seconds he was on his knees beside her, pulling Azure into his arms. "What happened?"

Azure buried her face in the safety of his arms. "Terrell…"

"Terrell?" Gavin pushed her back so he could look down into her face. "What did that bastard do? I'll kill him."

Azure was startled at his fierceness. "No, he didn't do anything to me."

"Just tell me what he did."

"Gavin." Even though seconds before she'd been blubbering like a baby, all Azure felt like doing now was laughing. She never would have thought Gavin had such a hero complex. "He didn't do anything to me. I promise."

"Then why are you crying?" Gavin seemed so confused at the concept of her crying just for the sake of crying. It was such a guy thing and Azure couldn't help but smile a little.

"Because I'm upset." Holding her hand up to keep him silent, Azure continued, "But not because of anything he directly did, but because of something he discovered."

With a reluctant sigh, Azure moved out of Gavin's arms and stood. Walking over to the dress still hanging on the dress form, Azure caressed it, knowing this was probably going to be one of the last times she touched it.

"I'm feeling completely lost here."

"Terrell was able to track down the descendants to whom the dress originally belonged."

"Isn't that what you wanted?"

"I did, but what I didn't want was for them to want the dress back."

"They want the dress back?" Gavin's gasp of surprise was almost similar to what Azure had uttered when she had talked to Meadow Lyncoln on the phone early this morning.

The older woman had burst into tears when Azure had phoned her to inquire more about the history of the dress. Instead of listening to a chronicle of the dress's past, Azure listened to Meadow's tearful encounter of the last time she had seen the dress. The very dress Meadow had worn in her wedding fifty odd years earlier and the very one she wanted her granddaughter to wear in her wedding this spring.

"Apparently the trunk was accidentally sold in an estate sale. Meadow said she would have never knowingly given it up for anything in the world." Brushing her hand against the soft fabric, Azure could see why. "She offered to reimburse me for the fee I paid Terrell as well as handle any shipping fees if I would send the dress back to her."

"I hope you told her what she could do with her money."

"Kind of." Azure smiled sadly. "I told her I would send her back the dress and she wouldn't have to pay anything."

"Send it back! Why would you do that?"

"Because it's the right thing to do."

"Azure, this makes no sense." To her surprise, Gavin looked almost more upset than she was. "You love that dress and more importantly, you own it. It's yours, so oh-fucking-well. You bought it fair and square. No court in the world would make you give it back."

"No one's making me give it back, Gavin."

"Then why are you doing it?"

Azure shrugged her shoulders, not sure how to explain to him that she just knew in her heart it was what she was supposed to do.

"I think everything happens for a reason."

"Everything?"

"Yes." Azure walked back over to the couch, taking his hand in hers as she sat. "Everything. For instance, if Jessie had been home that day, you would have never knocked on my door and *demi-pliéd* your way into my home or my heart."

"I still don't know what a *demi-plié* is." Gavin lovingly stroked her hand with his fingers. "But I know that I thank my lucky stars every day you let me in to your home and into your heart."

"Like you would have taken no for an answer."

"If Operation Charmin hadn't worked, I had a back-up plan."

"Stalker." She laughed as she leaned forward to brush a quick kiss on his lips. "The dress is the same way though. Just think, if I hadn't been perusing the store, I would have never had found the dress…"

"Which just goes to show you it's meant to be."

"It's meant for me to return it. I love history, and only someone with a love of the past would have taken the time to get as much information on the dress as they could which led me to Meadow who had been looking for the dress herself. I think I was supposed to find the dress so I could return it to her family."

"Azure, you love that dress."

"That I do." Azure glanced over at the dress. "But I need to do this."

"I don't agree, but if this is what you really truly feel you need to do, then I'll support your decision, begrudgingly."

"I appreciate it." She smiled. "I have to say, I'm very surprised you're this upset about it. I thought the dress being gone would make you feel better."

"Why in the world did you think that?"

Isn't it obvious? "I don't know, out of sight out of mind."

"Don't you know?" Gavin pulled Azure onto his lap. "I want you to have everything your heart desires."

"Gavin…" Azure was so touched by his words, for a moment she was speechless. When all else failed, she chose to say the one thing she'd been wanting to say for awhile. "I love you."

Gavin's grip around her tightened as he pulled her in closer to him and kissed her. The fierceness with which he held her told her all the feelings he had in his heart. But surprisingly, he was able to say the words as well. "I love you, too."

A comfortable silence drifted around them and Azure eased down in his arms until her head was resting against his chest. He made her feel so cherished, so loved.

"So when are you going to ship it to her?" Gavin asked.

"Actually, I was thinking of doing it today."

"Today!"

Azure sat up at his shocked tone. "Yes, why?"

"It's just too…" Gavin glanced over to the dress then back to Azure with a wicked gleam in his eyes. "I have an idea."

Azure warily asked, "What?"

"Let's make your dream dress a reality."

"What?"

"Let's get married. Right now."

"Married." Startled, Azure moved out of his arms and stood. Was he crazy? "Are you joking?"

"I've never been more serious in my life."

"But you don't want to get married."

"I'm allowed to change my mind."

"I'm…" Flabbergasted, Azure began to pace. "I know you think you're doing this because you think it's what I want."

"Are you saying you don't want to get married?"

"No, I'm saying I don't want to get married like this."

"Like what?" Gavin stood as well, a smile like none other she'd ever seen before on his face. "Like to the man you love, who loves you back."

"Just a few days ago we were talking about how you didn't want to get married."

"The other day I faced a cold, hard truth."

"What was that?"

"If I don't wise up I might lose you to some guy who's not nervous about getting married. You're a beautiful, wonderful woman, who any man would give his right arm just to have you smile at him the way you smile at me. Terrell was ready to kill me two days ago, just because you kissed me."

"He was not."

"He was, but that's not the point. I love you and I know I want to spend my life with you."

"I hear you, I really do. But I can't say yes."

Gavin's smile faded. "Why?"

"Because right now, you're doing this to make me feel better or because you don't want to lose me. Neither is a reason to get married."

"How about because I love you?"

"I love you too, but if we're meant to be, Gavin, it'll happen. With or without this dress."

Gavin pulled her into his arms. "Just so you know, I'm just as stubborn as you are. I won't stop asking."

"You better not."

"Are you sure you want to do this?"

Azure turned in his embrace so she could look at the dress. Suddenly, in the comfort of his arms, she wasn't as upset as she had been earlier. She loved the dress, she would have loved to wear it in her own wedding, but she didn't need it to make her wedding dream come true. "No, but I'm sure I have to. Besides you know the old saying, if you love something set it free…"

The dress was wonderful, but the man holding her was even better. He was the thing real dreams were made of, and he was all hers.

Epilogue

"Are you ready for bed?"

"Yes." The jubilant voice of her four-year-old daughter, Rose, never failed to make Azure smile. Sitting down on the bed next to her wasn't as easy as it used to be, but getting up was going to be a lot worse. It was a price she gladly paid to read to Rose before she went to sleep at night. Besides, Azure only had another three weeks with the extra weight of her unborn child in her womb to contend with anyway.

Looking down into the angelic face of her daughter, who had her mother's eyes but her father's wicked smile, never failed to bring tears to Azure's eyes. Like Gavin had promised her, he didn't relent with his marriage proposals, and one day she surprised them both by saying yes. It was a decision she'd never regretted in the wonderful six years that they'd been husband and wife. Their love had blossomed much like their ever-growing family.

"So, what do you want me to read to you tonight?"

"Nothing."

"Nothing?" Rose's words surprised her. Their nightly ritual had begun before her daughter had been old enough to know what a book was. "You don't want to hear a story tonight?"

"No, I do, but I don't want you to read me a story. I want you to tell me one."

The light dawned bright and clear. Azure knew exactly what Rose wanted. "About the wedding dress?"

"Yes."

"Okay." Azure settled back against the wall, getting herself ready for the tale Rose loved to hear. "Once upon a time, there was a magical dress. A wedding dress that had the amazing ability to bring love and happiness wherever it was.

"The dress was so special it was passed down from generation to generation, so that love and good fortune would continue to blossom for the Chandler clan, until one day…"

"The dress was sold by mistake." Rose interrupted, knowing the story almost verbatim.

"That's right, but luckily the dress was discovered by a…"

"A beautiful maiden, who was almost as lucky in love as the dress." Azure and Rose both looked up to see Gavin standing in the doorway, reciting the story with them. He walked over and dropped a quick kiss upon Rose's upturned lips. "Pardon me, Princess, for interrupting storytime, but it's one of my favorites."

"It's okay, Daddy, I like it too."

"So when the maiden…"

"Beautiful maiden," Rose corrected, earning a wink of approval from her father.

"Excuse me, beautiful maiden found the dress, she knew instinctively there was more to the dress than met the eye. She took it back to her castle where a handsome prince was waiting for her, beseeching entrance to her kingdom."

"And the beautiful maiden felt so bad for the twitching prince, that she granted him entrance." Rose looked to her father. "Daddy, why were you twitching?"

"Umm…I was really happy to meet your mom."

"Yes." Azure hid her laughter behind a cough. "The prince was so happy he even did a little dance."

"Azure…" Gavin growled.

"Anyway. The magical dress sensed that the couple, who were vastly different but so obviously destined to belong to one another, needed its help. So it wielded its enchanted spell on the unsuspecting couple. Who, of course, fell head over heels in love with each other. The only thing was, the dress didn't rightly belong to the maiden, and much to the prince's dismay, the kindhearted…"

"And beautiful," Rose and Gavin echoed.

"And beautiful maiden returned the magical dress to its rightful owners. As thanks, the gracious Lady Meadow granted the prince one wish, for the kind act his lady love had performed, and come the maiden's wedding day, the magical dress was hanging in her closet for her to wear, just like she'd dreamed it would be.

"Wearing the dress, the maiden strolled down the isle into the arms of her prince and the two were married, surrounded by love and magic. And they lived happily…"

"Ever after," Rose finished with a smile. "I love that story."

"I do too." Gavin held out his hand to Azure and gently helped her to her feet. "Now it's time for all little princesses to go to sleep. Night Rose."

"Night Daddy. Night Mommy."

Hand in hand, Azure and Gavin walked to the door, stopping only when Rose called out to them.

"Yes?" Azure asked, hand on the light switch.

"Do you think that one day I'll get married in the same magical dress you were married in?"

Azure smiled at her daughter. "If it's true love, then I can pretty much guarantee it."

Lena Matthews

Lena Matthews spends her days dreaming about handsome heroes and her nights with her own personal hero. Married to her college sweetheart, she is the proud mother of an extremely smart toddler, three evil dogs, and a mess of ants that she can't seem to get rid of.

When not writing she can be found reading, watching movies, lifting up the cushions on the couch to look for batteries for the remote control and plotting different ways to bring Buffy back on the air.

You can contact Lena through her website: www.lenamatthews.com

A Sixpence in
Her Shoe

Liz Andrews

Dedication

To Maggie Casper and Lena Matthews, I couldn't have done it without you ladies.

Chapter One

Damn, it happened again.

Melanie Parsons gazed around the large artifact room in horror. To anyone else's eyes it probably looked like an overgrown storage closet, but Melanie knew where every item was located. A large cavernous room, where all the artifacts were reviewed, researched and cataloged, and until displayed, stored there as well. The room was kept at a special temperature and had diffused lighting to ensure the items were well preserved. Long tables held numerous items in various states of the process. And she could plainly see the late nineteenth century cookware was missing. The iron skillets and pots, which she had been categorizing last night, were gone.

"Harold!" Melanie's screams brought a scurrying little man running from the adjacent room. His balding head glinted in the harsh lighting and Melanie wondered for the hundredth time why he had never gone for a corrective process. It was 2089 for Christ's sake. Hair re-growth was a minor procedure, one of many developed in the last fifty years. In fact, the practice had become so common doctors were offering "makeover specials" by the handful these days.

Her assistant, Harold Gill, came to a skidding halt in front of her. "Melanie, thank God you're here. I've contacted the police. We've been robbed."

Melanie restrained herself from rolling her eyes. Harold had a knack for stating the obvious.

"I can see that, Harold. What time did you get here? When did you contact them? Did they say how long it would be until they arrived?" Melanie slipped off her coat as she questioned him and strode toward the back room, with Harold hot on her heels.

"I arrived around seven this morning and immediately noticed the items missing. I contacted security and together we searched the room, but I knew we wouldn't find the cookware. You never take an item out of the artifact room until you're finished cataloging it. I told security, but since this was the second incident, they insisted we search. We didn't contact the police until after eight o'clock. They should be here any minute now." Harold was breathless by the time he finished speaking.

Melanie glanced at her watch and sighed with disgust. It was ten minutes after nine. The police obviously didn't think their burglary was a priority. She was sure if the message had come from some senator's office instead of the Smithsonian annex they would have gotten faster service. Unfortunately, history was dead to most Americans these days. It didn't have the prestige of science among the elite. Her department was regulated to the back rooms and bottom rungs of the ladder. Hanging up her coat, Melanie wondered if she should bother getting started on another cataloging project when the decision was made for her.

"Hello, anyone here?"

Finally, the police have arrived.

Melanie exited the office only to come to an abrupt halt, causing Harold, who had been following her, to run smack dab into her back. Losing her balance, Melanie pitched forward and was caught in the arms of a certifiable hunk. The man was six-foot-six and although muscular, he was certainly not fat. He had the swarthy good looks of someone with Latin descent. She gazed up into deep brown eyes that had an intensity she felt right to her core.

"Hey Torres, it looks as if you caught yourself something there. Gonna keep it or throw it back?"

Melanie gasped, suddenly realizing they had an audience. The man speaking was a few years older than she and good looking, but he couldn't hold a candle to the man who held her in his arms. Pulling away, she tried to regain her dignity.

"You okay Melanie? I'm sorry I ran into you. I wasn't expecting you to stop suddenly." Melanie turned at Harold's words, a forgiving smile on her face. Although he often frustrated her to no end, the accident had been her own fault.

"It's okay Harold, I'm fine." Returning her attention back to the two agents, she continued. "I was expecting the police, not the UAS."

The United Americas Securities, or UAS for short, was created thirty years earlier when North and South America formed the United Americas Coalition. The various countries realized they needed one united security force to compete globally with the European Union.

"Yes ma'am, the D.C. police contacted us as soon as they received your report this morning. Especially since this is the second burglary this month." The other agent was the one who spoke, but Melanie couldn't keep her gaze off her rescuer. The microfiber of his uniform clung to him like a second skin. She had to literally shake herself out of a daydream to respond to the other man.

"Did the report tell you it was only a skillet and pots stolen? It's not as if this burglary was a terrorist plot." Melanie's defensiveness was apparent in her tone, which was unfortunate. She always tried to act properly, at least in public, and questioning those in authority was not proper. Although she had been wishing for prompt attention by the police, she didn't think the burglaries were serious enough for the UAS to get involved.

"Yes ma'am, we know what was stolen. But there's a certain pattern here we're investigating. The report indicates all the items stolen are from the same approximate time period. We think it may be Traditionalists." The agent paused dramatically, as if waiting for some sort of reaction, but everyone in the room remained silent. A snort accompanied the agent's next words. "Of course, Torres here doesn't believe it."

Melanie's eyes widened and her glance flew to Agent Torres. His face was grim, as if he had heard the gibe more than once.

"I think we need to investigate before we make any rash judgments." His voice was dark and smooth as molasses. Melanie shivered, even though the room was kept at ideal temperature conditions.

"Speaking of investigating, what exactly do you need from me?" Melanie tried to return the conversation back to the task at hand and banish her reveries of the agent.

Agent Torres glanced down her body as if slowly undressing her with his eyes. Melanie had to resist raising her hands to shield herself from his gaze. She squinted for a moment, wondering if he had the new X-ray contacts, but then decided she was just being imaginative.

Although the technology allowing someone to look through a person's clothes directly to their body had been around for hundreds of years, it was only recently a company had come out with the new portable devices. Unfortunately for them, most people didn't wear contacts or glasses anymore because of the advances in medical technology, so when someone did wear those items it was usually an obvious sign the person was using the new contacts.

"I'll need to see your records on the items stolen." Melanie could have sworn Agent Torres looked almost disappointed when Harold offered to get the records for him. She watched for a moment as they both disappeared into the office.

"I'm sorry ma'am, I never did introduce myself. I'm Agent Randall Miko."

"Nice to meet you. My name is Melanie Parsons and I run the historical artifacts department."

The agent briefly tapped his earpiece and the hologram of a keyboard and computer appeared before him. "Just let me get some information from you." He began typing away at the phantom keys. His questions continued, even after Harold and Agent Torres returned from the back office.

"Do you have any leads on the case? Is there any chance you'll be able to retrieve our items?" Melanie knew she had a tendency to fire off questions when she was nervous or upset and today definitely qualified as a day where both of those attributes applied.

"We can't release any information as of yet, but we'll certainly let you know if we find your stuff." Agent Miko had finally completed all of his questions and shut down the portable computing device. Melanie assumed the system was similar to the one she used and the information, digitally stored in the earpiece, would be downloaded to the main system when he returned to his own office.

"Yes, I'll hopefully be seeing you very soon." Agent Torres's comments sounded much more personal and Melanie couldn't help but shiver again at the image it evoked in her mind. She needed to pull herself together.

"Well, thank you for your time and coming out here. We need to get back to work."

Agent Torres gave her another scorching look as both agents left, promising to notify her if any of the missing items turned up. Although it had been a memorable morning, there was still work to be done. Melanie turned to Harold as she literally and figuratively rolled up her sleeves. "Okay Harold, let's get to work."

Regrettably they barely got started before being interrupted.

"Melanie, what's this I hear about a burglary? Are you causing trouble again?"

Melanie sighed inwardly at the sight of her boss, Stan Johnson, walking toward them. The man looked like an angel, with blond hair and blue eyes, but he had the heart of a devil. He was constantly finding ways to make her life miserable.

"Oh Mr. Johnson, it was awful. I came in this morning and immediately saw the items missing." Harold continued to relay the entire story to Stan in the most dramatic manner possible.

At the end of Harold's litany, Stan turned viciously on her. "Melanie, this is completely unacceptable. You're taking entirely too long to catalog the items."

"Perhaps we should discuss this in my office." Melanie didn't think it appropriate to argue in front of Harold, but Stan seemed to have no compunction on the matter.

"No, we'll discuss this right here and now. If you weren't completing this project at a snail's pace this whole incident would have never occurred."

"Just how do you figure?" Sarcasm dripped from her voice. She couldn't disguise her disgust for the man and stopped attempting to do so many months ago.

"If you didn't spend so much time on this boring stuff and just did a cursory review, the cataloging would be done by now and all these items would be in storage. Instead we're backed up to kingdom come with no end in sight."

Melanie knew Stan considered old west items boring because they weren't in the political spotlight right now. Everyone was intrigued with the late twentieth century instead. "Look Stan, I work at a pace to get the job done right and I'm not going to cut corners just because you think this period is boring. Everything needs to be cataloged correctly and as far as being in storage, that's a joke. *This* is storage. You know we don't have the luxury of more space right now."

"You think you're so high and mighty." Stan sneered at her. "We'll just see how much funding you get when it goes public you can't keep items secure."

Melanie held back the angry retort that immediately came to mind. It would do no good to argue with Stan because, in his mind, he was always right. Melanie had been given the job of department head over him three years earlier, and although Stan was the big boss now, he still couldn't let the old slight go. He constantly picked at everything she did, trying to make her look bad. He didn't even get the director's position by merit, but through an appointment by one of his cronies.

Stan paused for a moment, awaiting her reply before stalking off in disappointment, muttering under his breath with a sneer. "No more than what I should expect from a member of a *Traditionalist* family."

Melanie tried not to let his comments bother her. Although she didn't always subscribe to the viewpoints of her family, she loved them all fiercely and usually defended them vigorously. But she knew Stan was deliberately baiting her. He would be extremely happy if she responded, and Melanie did everything in her power to make sure she never did anything to make Stan happy.

"Oh Melanie, I'm sorry. If I knew it was going to get you in trouble I never would have contacted security this morning." Harold's forlorn apology touched Melanie. He really was a nice guy.

"Don't worry about it Harold. You did the right thing." Melanie patted his hand as they returned to work.

CR&O

Melanie kicked off her shoes and pulled off her panty hose as soon as she walked in the back door of her house. Reaching up, she removed the clip holding her hair in place and let her tresses fall. It had been a long, arduous day, made worse not only by the burglary, but also by the attack of her boss on her character. She tried to forget about work, but unfortunately her usual tricks weren't working. The music she ordered to play in the background should have been soothing, as well as the glass of wine she was sipping, but she was still on edge.

Setting the glass down on the counter, Melanie contemplated dinner. She was too tired to cook, but knew it wasn't good for her health to continue skipping meals. The stress of working for Stan was really getting to her, even affecting her away from the office. It was probably time to start looking for a new job, but unfortunately there wasn't a lot of work for historical curator types outside the Smithsonian.

The doorbell chime almost had her knocking her glass off the kitchen counter. Her nerves were definitely shot. Melanie lived in an old brownstone in the Arlington area of Washington D.C. and liked the entire low-tech atmosphere of her building. Of course, she had a state of the art security system, but no video surveillance for her. The idea of turning a historical house into a technical palace just didn't seem right to her. It would ruin the ambiance of living in the old building.

Strolling toward the front entrance, Melanie glanced through the peephole before opening the door.

"Well, well, well, if it isn't Agent Torres." Melanie stepped back and let Brady into the living room. "Did you come to tuck me into bed?"

Chapter Two

Brady waited until Melanie shut the door before he turned and pulled her in his arms. "Aren't you the little tease? I've been thinking about getting you back in my arms all day. And not with an audience around this time."

Melanie smiled and wrapped her arms around his neck. Brady had to force himself to concentrate on her words when all he really wanted to do was enjoy the soft body pressed against his own. "I was shocked when I walked out of my office and saw you standing there."

"So shocked you threw yourself into my arms." Brady felt the need to constantly tease Melanie because she always acted prim and proper. He wanted her to let go and explore all those wild inhibitions he could sense just under the surface.

"That was all Harold's fault," Melanie protested, surprisingly going along with his banter. "If not for him you wouldn't have gotten to cop a feel so easily."

"*Cop a feel?* Don't tell me you're jumping on the twentieth century bandwagon."

"I heard it today on the satellite cast and thought it very apt. You are part of the security force after all."

"Maybe I need to take you downtown and make sure you're telling me the truth. We have ways of making you talk, you know."

Brady ran his hands down her back to cup her ass through the material of her skirt. Staring into Melanie's big blue eyes, he saw them glaze over at both his words and his touch. She was damn pretty, with rioting red curling hair. At work she scraped it back, trying to tame it, but Brady loved it when she took her hair down and let it go wild. Melanie had curves in all the right places, with breasts that were more than a handful and a fine rounded ass.

He and Melanie had been dating for the last two months and they both had held back on taking the final step of sleeping together. If only he dared to take their loving to the next level. Unfortunately, he still wasn't sure if Melanie would be willing. Brady was a man who loved to be in control, both in the bedroom and out it. He wasn't willing to have another vanilla relationship, but knew he wouldn't be able to keep his tendencies under wraps once they started sleeping together. Recently, he thought he had seen signs Melanie would be willing to take that step, but it was nothing they had discussed.

"How would you make me talk?" Melanie's husky question surprised the hell out of Brady, but he wasn't one to look a gift horse in the mouth. If she wanted to play the game, he was more than willing to show her the ropes. It was if she had just been reading his mind. He just hoped he was reading her signals right.

"Well first, I'd make sure you couldn't get away." Reaching down, Brady grabbed his security cuffs off his belt loop. He knew he could be making a big mistake here, but he lived by the philosophy that a person needed to take chances when they came their way. Brady's body, heart and mind were telling him this was a once in a lifetime opportunity.

"I'm pretty strong. If I wanted to fight you, how would you subdue me?" If Brady thought Melanie was teasing him, he would have backed down in a second. But all the signs were apparent she was looking forward to whatever he had to teach her. She was breathing heavily and licking her lips as if in anticipation. Brady could imagine Melanie using her mouth on him in numerous ways. His cock, responding to his wayward thoughts, pushed at the confines of his uniform pants.

"Like this." Brady swiftly turned her in his arms, grasping her arms and pulling them behind her. He snapped the security cuffs on her wrists before she even finished her gasp.

"Hmm, that was pretty sneaky of you. But you still need to get me to talk."

Brady turned Melanie around, needing to see her face, to make sure she was okay with where this night seemed to be heading. Pushing her back against the door, he pressed his hips against hers, allowing her to feel his straining erection. Melanie's eyes were wide and her breath came in short gasps. Her nipples were hard as they tented the fabric of her blouse.

"Even though I never would hurt you, I just might have to see how much you could take before you would talk." Brady was still trying to come to terms with what was going on here. It was if his fantasies and reality had suddenly collided. They had never talked about their sexual proclivities, but he wouldn't have pegged Melanie as a closet submissive. Yet here she was, egging him on. He hoped she was serious and not just playing some kind of twisted game.

"I think I could take a lot from you, Agent Torres." Even though Melanie's hands were restrained behind her back, she found a way to touch him. She pressed her hips into his and rubbed her breasts against his chest. Whispering into his ear she added, "Why don't you try me out," as she gently bit his lobe.

Before Melanie could change her mind, Brady leaned down and flipped her over his shoulder, with her head hanging down over his back and her ass in the air. Holding her tight around the legs he turned toward the stairs, mounting them swiftly. Stopping abruptly, he realized he had no idea which room was hers.

"Last door on the right."

It was as if Melanie knew just what he was thinking. Wordlessly moving down the hall, Brady found the room she indicated.

"Lights on low," Melanie ordered and lights immediately illuminated the room at the dim level she indicated. A large Shaker style bed dominated the room.

She must be from a moneyed family to have so many antique pieces of furniture.

Lightly dropping her on the bed, Brady knelt beside her, staring down into her face. He knew he was probably crazy, but he had to make sure she understood what she was doing.

"Is this really what you want? I need to know."

Melanie smiled then and nodded her head shyly. Her face was blazing, but her voice was steady. "I want you to dominate me, Brady. I didn't want our first sexual experience together to be a lie. I want...no, I need this."

That was all Brady needed to know. They could talk later about the details, but for now, he needed this as much as she did. "Okay, baby, I'll give us both just what we need. But if you get scared, or need me to stop, you say...'history'." The one thing he had learned was the importance of having a safe word in a dominant relationship. It helped clear up a lot of potential misunderstanding later down the road.

Melanie nodded, but Brady wanted to make sure she knew what to say. "No, tell me."

"If I need you to stop or want to take a break I have to say 'history'."

"Good girl. Now roll over." Melanie immediately rolled to her side and Brady released the cuffs. They didn't go far though since he had plans for them later. "How do you feel?" Brady asked as he gently rubbed Melanie's arms and wrists, returning circulation to the limbs.

"Okay. Excited. Nervous."

"Those are all good feelings, baby. Just remember, if it doesn't feel good, you let me know."

"I will." Melanie sat up and clutched at his shoulders. "Do you realize we haven't even kissed tonight?"

Brady chuckled at her blatant come-on. Who was he to turn down such an offer? Bending his head, he pressed his lips to hers, gently easing her mouth open with gradual pressure and slipping his tongue inside. She tentatively met him, move for move, their tongues dueling in a mating dance. Melanie loved to kiss and drive Brady crazy, but he wasn't going to let her distract him, not tonight.

Breaking the kiss, Brady fought to catch his breath. "Lie back on the bed, grasp the headboard and don't let go."

Melanie lay back as ordered and reached above her head to take a spindle in each hand. The movement drew her breasts up, as if offering them to Brady. He swiftly unbuttoned the silky material of her blouse, baring her breasts to his gaze. The cups of her bra were sheer and he could see her dark areolas and nipples through the material. Exposed to the night air and his gaze, her nipples were hard little points.

Brady cupped each breast, one per hand, enjoying the feel of the soft flesh. He had tasted her breasts before, but never had they looked as sweet as tonight. Leaning down, he circled a nipple with his tongue before sucking it into his mouth, fabric and all. Melanie groaned and arched her back, straining to push herself more fully into his mouth. But as ordered she continued to hold onto the headboard.

Releasing the nipple with an audible pop, Brady turned his attention to the other breast. He pinched the nipple between his thumb and index finger and then rolled it back and forth, watching the little nub of flesh engorge with blood at his ministrations. Melanie whimpered, but again pushed her chest toward his questing fingers as if begging for more. Her eyes were closed, but the look on her face was one of pure ecstasy.

Leaning down, Brady soothed the tortured nipple with a swipe of his tongue. "You don't have to be quiet, baby. Tell me what you like, how it feels. I want to know everything."

Her eyes flew open at his words. "Oh God, Brady. It's so much. The feelings are…too intense for words, but at the same time, it's still not enough. I want more."

Cupping her breasts again, Brady lightly ran his thumb back and forth across her nipples, continuing to tease her. "You're very sensitive here. Have you ever thought about getting pierced?" Brady could just imagine driving her to climax with nipple stimulation alone. His cock, already painfully aching, jerked at the thought.

"Yes, but I've always been too scared. I've heard the sensations are wonderful though."

"I'd love to see you pierced. But I don't know if I could keep my hands off during the healing process." Brady continued to taunt and tease, rolling and pinching her nipples as she writhed on the bed.

Finally allowing her respite, Brady sat back for a moment to view the magnificent sight. Melanie was still gripping the spindles of the headboard tightly, her breasts straining against the sheer fabric of her bra. Her movements on the bed had caused her skirt to ruck up her legs, exposing her thighs and just a hint of her panties underneath.

"Let go of the headboard and sit up here for a minute."

Melanie slowly released the headboard, flexing her fingers for a moment before sitting up. Brady helped her slip her blouse off and then turned her slightly to release the hooks of her bra. Tossing the garments to the side, Brady turned Melanie back toward him, sweeping her fiery hair away from her face. "Still okay?"

He worried he was pushing her too hard, too fast. Although she said she wanted this, Brady had the feeling this was her first encounter of dominance. And truth be told, most of his encounters had been mild experiments of his own. In fact, he had only been in one long-term dominant relationship before.

"You're not chickening out on me already, are you?" Melanie smiled and stroked his face.

"Not on your life. Now stand up." Brady stood and helped her up, turning her so she stood in front of him, her back to his front. He swept her hair back, exposing her neck, and leaned down to lick the sensitive area behind her ear. Grasping her waistband he unhooked her skirt, letting the material fall to the floor.

"I'd love to see you in some thigh-high stockings or garters and heels. Lying spread eagle on the bed and tied down, helpless to move. Then I'd run my hands up your silky legs to your sweet pussy, soaked with cream."

Melanie moaned at his words and ground her hips back against his erection. "Would you lick me?"

"Not at first. I'd tease you a bit, until I had you dripping on the bed. Then I'd part your folds and discover all your hidden treasures. And just when you were ready to come I'd stop for a moment and then bring you back to your peak, over and over again until you were begging for me to let you come."

Brady parted her thighs as he spoke, pulling her legs apart, exposing her dampened panties to his questing fingers. He rubbed her clit through the material. She tried to close her legs and trap his hand tight against her, but he wasn't going to allow her to get away with trying to be in control. He wanted to decide when and how she would come.

"Someone is being a very bad girl." Brady pulled his hand from between her thighs and hooking his fingers in the material of her panties he pulled them down her legs.

"What?" Melanie shook herself from her passion-induced haze, seemingly unable to comprehend his words or actions.

"Who is in control of your body, Melanie?" Brady wanted her to realize just what his form of dominance meant. He would control every aspect of their sexual relationship and she needed to understand that now, before things went any further.

"You are."

"And who decides how and when you come?"

"You do."

"That's right. I think you need a small punishment just as a reminder. Get on the bed, on all fours."

Melanie quickly scrambled onto the bed, arranging herself just as he requested.

"Do you remember your word?"

"Yes." Although low, her voice was still strong. Brady was sure she wasn't necessarily scared, probably just a bit worried about the unknown.

"Widen your legs for me." Melanie did as he ordered and Brady reached out and stroked a finger through her slit, gathering the moisture there and bringing it to his lips to lick. "You taste heavenly."

Melanie glanced over her shoulder, watching him as he licked his finger. She had a little Mona Lisa smile playing about her lips and Brady knew, even though she didn't know what exactly was going to happen next, she was ready for it.

Chapter Three

Melanie couldn't believe she was kneeling on her bed, awaiting a spanking from Brady. One of her most persistent, all-time fantasies was coming to life right before her eyes. She trembled from the force of the realization of what was about to happen.

"Lower your head."

Brady's order had her panting for more. Why his orders made her willing to bend over and spread her legs she had no idea. Usually when someone tried to order her around it made her hackles rise. But the need to be sexually dominated was her secret, one she had only most recently admitted to herself.

Melanie lowered her head as ordered and waited to see what Brady did next. This whole evening had spiraled out of her control as soon as she had thrown caution to the wind. She'd sensed Brady might be the one to fulfill her desires, but until tonight she had never been willing to bare her soul so completely.

The time seemed to stretch interminably as Melanie waited for Brady to do something, anything.

Smack

The swat on her ass wasn't painful. But the surprise of the blow pushed her body forward and Melanie almost lost her balance. Preparing for another smack Melanie was shocked when Brady caressed her, covering her heated ass with the hand that caused the burn.

"Did you enjoy that?"

Melanie nodded shakily, but apparently Brady wasn't satisfied with her non-verbal communication.

"Tell me, what did you like?"

"I don't know, I just liked it."

"Was it the spank you liked more or the fact you gave up control?"

"I...uh, I liked both."

Brady chuckled, but didn't say any more. Once again he dipped his hand into her cream. Stroking, he brought the moisture back towards her rosette, rubbing back and forth, but never penetrating her. Melanie gasped at his caresses, trembling at the force of her reaction. She wanted to scream at him to push his finger inside her, although she had never desired anal sex in her life.

"Not tonight, but soon. I'll take you there. And you'll take me, deep inside."

Melanie moaned at the picture he was painting in her mind. She could see herself, as if watching a movie, with Brady behind her and buried in her ass, thrusting deep as he stimulated her clit. Pushing back against his teasing finger she groaned as he pushed the tip inside her.

"I can see you like the idea, sweetie, but we'll have to work our way up to this." Brady slipped his finger free and patted her upturned ass. "Unfortunately we still have your punishment to finish. I won't be distracted this easily."

Melanie could hear Brady step back and braced herself for the next blow. He didn't disappoint, landing his first swat within seconds. Alternating the blows, first on the right and then left cheek, he methodically spanked Melanie's ass until it felt as if it were on fire. Brady stopped for a moment, his breathing ragged.

"I can't stand anymore, please Brady, fuck me." Melanie couldn't believe the words coming from her mouth. She never begged. But she was begging now and she didn't care. She craved completion. He controlled her, dominated her, punished her and now she needed him to fuck her.

"Who's in charge?"

"You are." Melanie lifted her head, turning her pleading gaze towards him. "Please."

"Lucky for you, I'm in agreement."

Brady pulled her upright until she was kneeling on the bed, looking him in the eye. She realized at some point, while she was on all fours, Brady had stripped and he now stood before her naked. Unbelievably she'd never heard him, too wrapped up in the sensations he evoked in her.

Glancing down, Melanie noted Brady wasn't unaffected by their love play. His erection was dripping pre-cum, the silky liquid dragging across her belly. She reached out to grasp him as if drawn to a flame.

Brady gasped as her hand closed around his pulsing cock. It was warm and throbbed with the beat of his heart.

"Can I taste you?" Melanie instinctively knew she should ask and felt a warm glow as he nodded his approval.

Sliding off the bed, Melanie sank to the floor in front of him. She licked up his shaft and back down again, tasting him. He had a clean musky scent that made her crave more. Moving her lips up his cock, she allowed the tip to slide into her mouth. Just holding the head, she sucked hard, flicking her tongue around the slit at the top.

"Yeah, just like that." Brady grasped her hair, wrapping it in his hands. He didn't push her face onto his cock or pull harshly, which encouraged her further. Melanie rarely performed oral sex, usually finding no man was worth the effort, and most were downright assholes about it, basically trying to fuck her face. But Brady seemed very appreciative of her endeavor and she figured he was probably just the type who would return the favor—a true rarity.

Sucking his cock more fully into her mouth, Melanie reached up and cupped Brady's balls, squeezing ever so gently. He moaned in appreciation, his hips jerking toward her. She coated his shaft with saliva, easily sliding his cock in and out her mouth. The grip on her hair tightened and his hips were pumping in rhythm to her movements. Melanie lightly raked her teeth over the head of his cock and Brady shouted hoarsely, pulling back from her.

"That was great baby, but I don't want to come in your mouth. I want to come in your sweet pussy. Do you have protection?"

"I have inhalers in the drawer." Grabbing the combination birth control and disease prevention inhalers, they both quickly took a puff of the drug that would protect them for the next twenty four hours.

Pulling her up, Brady briefly kissed her before pushing her back toward the bed. Melanie lay on her back, arms above her head. Although she wouldn't ask, she wanted to feel restrained when they had sex for the first time. As if reading her mind, Brady grabbed the security cuffs he'd used earlier. Pressing a button on the side, the cuffs expanded, so they could be looped around a couple of the spindles of the headboard. This allowed Melanie to have her hands slightly apart while still being locked into place with just one pair of cuffs. She was pretty sure they hadn't been invented for this purpose, however. The thought made her giggle.

"So you think this is funny, huh?"

Melanie decided she wanted to play. Blinking her eyes, she lowered her voice sexily. "Oh, Agent Torres, you've got me in a *very* precarious situation. What do you plan to do with me?"

Brady knelt on the bed between her legs, slowly pushing them apart. Gently massaging her calves, he stroked his way up her legs to her inner thighs. Melanie's breath hitched as he reached the apex, but then he abruptly stopped, keeping his hands on either side of her pussy.

"Well Miss Parsons, you do seem to have yourself in a very sticky situation. As to what I have planned, hmmm, there are so many possibilities. I really want to eat this sweet cream I see your pussy drowning in, but I don't know if you deserve such a treat. Besides, I don't think I can wait until I fuck you. We'll have to take a rain check on that, okay?"

"Okay." Melanie's response was breathy, barely a whisper. Although she'd love to experience his brand of oral sex, she was just as anxious as him, anticipating the sex between them. She had a feeling she would have many future nights at Brady's tender mercy.

Brady leaned over her, kissing her mouth hungrily, twining his tongue with hers in an intricate dance. Breaking the kiss, she watched as he sat back and fought to regain his breath. Reaching down, he cupped her breasts, kneading softly and pinching her nipples before rolling them between his thumb and finger. Her hips arched off the bed at the stimulation. Melanie could feel his cock dripping pre-cum and rubbing against her skin. She wanted to beg him to fuck her before she went insane with longing.

"I won't lie and tell you I'll be gentle. It's been a long night and my control is at the breaking point."

"Take me Brady, please. It's what I want too."

Positioning his cock against her sex, Brady slid in, her body opening and accepting him with one thrust. For an instant she thought time had stopped. She had been waiting for this moment for what seemed like an eternity and now he was finally inside her.

Brady began fucking her slowly, with long, measured strokes, pulling almost all the way out before plunging in again, filling her up completely.

"Fuck me hard, Brady, please." She didn't care if she was begging.

Pulling back, Brady began thrusting harder, pushing her legs up until they were practically hanging over his shoulders. Her clit, super sensitive at this point, vibrated with his every downstroke. He was able to sink into her even deeper in this position, hitting a place she never knew existed. Her body rocked with shockwaves of pleasure as she orgasmed.

Slowly lowering her legs, Brady sped up his plunges. Melanie tightened her vaginal muscles, wanting to give him as much pleasure as he had given her. His moans grew louder as he stiffened and ejaculated inside her before collapsing in a heap. Melanie lay there, her legs restlessly stroking the backs of his thighs, wishing for this one moment her hands were free and she could touch him.

Eventually regaining his composure, Brady rolled off her and sat up. Stretching above her head, he released the security cuffs and gently massaged her arms.

"Are you okay?"

"More than okay, I feel wonderful." Melanie reached up and stroked his face, amazed by the look of relief she saw there.

"Stay right here, I'm going to get you cleaned up." Brady hopped off the bed and was out of the room before she could tell him where the bathroom was located. She could hear him opening a couple of doors before he eventually found it.

Returning quickly, Brady pressed a warm washcloth against her well-used flesh, cleaning the evidence of their encounter. Pulling back the covers, he tucked her into bed before returning to the bathroom. She felt loved and cherished by this man. Melanie hoped she wasn't reading more into this night than just a happy man who was excited he finally got some. The uncertainty of the other person's reaction was one of the reasons she'd never revealed her desire to be dominated. Relationships were hard enough without the added pressures of her particular cravings.

As Brady returned to her room for the second time, Melanie sat up, propped against her pillows and the headboard behind her. Sitting on the edge of the bed, he looked at her intently for a moment.

"Are you tired?"

Melanie thought about his question a moment before answering. "A little sore, but tired in a good way, like when I've exercised. Why?"

"I was wondering if you were up to talking for a bit."

"Sure, what did you want to talk about?" Scooting over she made room for Brady to join her on the bed.

"I was wondering about those burglaries."

Melanie's mind tried to wrap around the words coming out his mouth. Worried they were going to have the big relationship talk, she was shocked by his thought process.

She had the best sex of her life and he wanted to talk about work. *Ugh, men!*

"So what about the burglaries?" Fine, she was willing to play this game for awhile—be the little woman who asked her man about his day.

"We're never going to catch these guys unless we set a trap for them. And I think I've got the perfect bait."

"Really?" Melanie was surprised. Brady had never seemed very interested in historical artifacts before.

"It just so happens I know a woman who has a dress from the very time period the thieves seem to be interested in. Think I might convince her to let me use said dress?"

Melanie's eyes narrowed. She didn't know how he'd found out about the dress, but her radar was going off double time.

"What do you know about dresses?" Maybe she could bluff her way through this.

"Come on Melanie, I've seen it. When I was looking for the bathroom I opened the room next door and saw the dress hanging there, wrapped in the special polymer you use to preserve old stuff. And I saw the date on the tag you had attached, 1878."

Melanie's heart clenched at the thought he'd seen the dress. Although she shied away from her family's traditionalist values, it was the one thing from her childhood she'd brought with her when she moved from home. The dress represented all the things she thought she abhorred about the historical role of women, but in her heart she loved it. It was a bit embarrassing Brady had found out two of her biggest secrets in one night.

"That dress is a family heirloom. I can't just hand it over to you to use as bait in some scheme."

"It's not *some* scheme."

"Brady, did I ever tell you the history of the dress?"

"No." Although only one word it held a wealth of emphasis and Melanie could almost hear Brady's question, "what did the history of a dress have to do with their conversation?"

"It was a very modern dress for its time. Matilda Chandler was a mail order bride and her mother made the dress so she could have a real wedding. Afterwards, she wrote letters to her children, telling them about the need to preserve the history of their family and her outlook on love. Other letters were written by the women in the family who wore the dress and passed down through the generations."

"We actually lost the dress and letters for a time early in this century. But a lovely young woman found them and, after reading the letters, she did everything in her power to find the family and send them back to us. And if I lose the dress now…"

"Do you trust me?"

Melanie squirmed as she considered his question. She'd just allowed him to restrain and spank her, giving up complete control to him. Could she trust him outside the bedroom as well?

She sighed heavily before replying. "Yes, I trust you. But I still don't see what trust has to do with anything."

"If you trust me then you've got to realize I'd never do anything to hurt you or the dress."

"I suppose."

"You suppose right. It's getting late, we better get some sleep. Lights off," Brady ordered and although she hadn't invited him, he snuggled down into the bed, pulling her back against him and wrapping his arms around her. "Besides, I noticed it's a wedding dress according to the tag and you might need it in the future."

Chapter Four

Brady walked into UAS headquarters the next morning, feeling mighty satisfied. Spending the night with Melanie had been all he'd hoped for and more. After she fell asleep, he lay cradling her in his arms, with a feeling he'd never experienced seeping into his heart and soul. At thirty-three he had given up on finding a woman who was sexually compatible with him in the bedroom and intellectually compatible with him everywhere else.

Not that he'd be limiting his sexual interactions with Melanie to the bedroom.

"Well, well, well. Looks like Torres got laid last night. Who is she and can you tell any stories?"

Brady sobered instantly. He didn't know his new partner, Randall Miko, too well yet and certainly wasn't planning to share any stories with him. Hell, he hadn't even told the man he was steadily dating anyone.

"What's up, Miko?"

"No stories?" Randall lifted his eyebrows, laughter playing over his face. "Okay, fine, work it is. Take a look at this."

Randall walked over to his desk, bringing something up on his holo-monitor. As Brady approached the desk he saw a still hologram of Melanie's workroom, with a shot of her frozen in time.

"What's this?"

"Play back date/time stamped zero, three, seventeen, two thousand eighty nine, seventeen eleven."

The hologram began to play.

Brady watched as Melanie pulled on her coat and picked up her purse. "Harold, I'm heading out, only ten minutes late." Melanie began walking through the large room and Harold, who had been out of the picture at the beginning of the shot, stepped into view.

"Have a good time tonight, Melanie."

Melanie looked startled for a moment. "How did you know I was going out?"

Harold's blush could easily be seen in the holo-picture. "I overheard your side of the conversation about going out to dinner at *Ma Moitié*. Are you going for a girl's night?" Harold had a hopeful look on his face.

"No actually, it's a date." Melanie waved good-bye and they continued to watch as Harold finished putting items away, his head lowered in dejection.

Brady winced slightly. He had taken Melanie to the new French restaurant for their third date. It was also the first time he had an inkling there might be something more between them.

"As interesting as this is, what are we looking for?" By now Harold had also left and they were staring at an empty room.

"Wait for it. I wanted you to see the beginning so you knew the difference."

Suddenly a bright light flashed on the screen, blinding them for a moment.

"Forward twenty." The screen jumped forward twenty minutes, staying brilliant for a few more minutes before suddenly returning to normal.

"Okay, I saw the bright light. What does it mean? I don't see a difference."

"These are the security vids from the night of the first burglary. I compared them to the ones two nights ago and the exact same phenomena occurred in both vids. The techies speculate the bright light was a low level electro-magnetic pulse that knocked out the surveillance equipment for approximately twenty-five minutes.

"It would have to be pretty minimal. Did it affect any other equipment?"

"Not that we can tell so far. This was a very specific job. They didn't care if someone knew when they were there, they just didn't want to be identified."

Randall shut down the security vid as Brady sat down at the desk directly across from him.

"I still don't see why we're even involved in this. There aren't any leads tying these burglaries specifically to the Traditionalists and certainly not to the Purists. Would Purists even use an EM pulse?"

Purists were a radical splint cell group of Traditionalists that had eschewed all modern technology, to the point they lived in communes out in the middle of nowhere. They had protested numerous times on Capital Hill, asking that their *nation* be recognized as sovereign from the United Americas. Unfortunately, Purists had also been linked to a number of terrorist events, usually minor acts that caused more nuisance than injury or harm.

"Who else would want a bunch of pots and pans?" Randall rolled his eyes and then groaned. "Heads-up, boss man is coming this way."

Brady turned to see Captain William Turner bearing straight for them. Although he always seemed to have a permanent scowl on his face, he looked particularly pissed off today at something—or someone.

"Torres, in my office now." Captain Turner kept walking, right past them and headed toward the office at the end of the hall. Randall stood up when Brady got to his feet and the captain turned for a moment. "I didn't request you, Miko, so sit your ass back down." The captain turned back, swiftly walking towards his office.

Randall immediately sat, shock written all over his face. "Damn, you must be in a pile of shit up to your nose. Good luck man."

Brady had no idea what the problem could be so he didn't even waste time trying to speculate. He'd find out soon enough. Reaching the captain's office he knocked briefly before entering, closing the door behind him and standing at attention in front of the desk.

"Do you even know who you're fucking?"

Of all the things the captain could have said, this was the one thing Brady wasn't expecting.

"Excuse me sir, but I have no idea what you mean."

"Well, let me enlighten you. Melanie Parsons, of the Philadelphia Parsons, comes from one of the biggest Traditionalist families in this country.

Her family goes back to the wild, wild west of the 1800s. Is this starting to ring any bells for you?"

Brady stood in shock. His little Modernist was from a Traditionalist family? And a rich one it seemed. Melanie had often spoken of her family, but she had never given this kind of detail before. It suddenly explained so much. Why she had a historical wedding dress hanging in her house for one thing.

"You seem a bit surprised, Torres. Didn't your girlfriend tell you her family was in opposition to our government? In fact, her father just offered a hundred thousand dollar donation to the campaign of any Traditionalist who runs against a Modernist in the upcoming election. In any election in the United Americas. That's a hell of a lot of money, son."

Brady didn't care what Melanie's family did or who her father contributed money to. And he would deal with her keeping secrets later. Instead he decided to focus in on the one thing he could deal with right now.

"Are you having me followed?"

The captain looked up at Brady's question and laughed. "Have you been listening to me? I just told you your girlfriend and her family are raging Traditionalists, you're investigating radical Traditionalist groups and all you can ask me is if we're following you?"

"Sir, Article 71 of the United Americas revised code clearly states that all members of the UAS must be informed if they are to be put under surveillance unless they are directly suspected of a criminal act. So I ask you again, are you having me followed?" Brady was barely holding on to his temper. If they suspected him of a criminal act his career was over.

"Now don't get torqued, Torres. We've been following the Parsons woman and the agent at her house last night recognized you. He immediately came to me, so there are no worries this will get around. But we've got a real problem here. You can't continue this investigation if you're personally involved with one of the suspects."

"Melanie's a suspect?"

"She had access to the items stolen and she comes from a Traditionalist family, so of course she's a suspect."

"Sir, I know for a fact she is incapable of this. Besides, she was with me the night of the first burglary."

"She may be working with other members of a group. You can't assume just because you're fucking her she's innocent."

Brady took a menacing step forward. "If you insult her one more time I won't be responsible for my actions, *sir*."

"Stand down, Torres, or you just might find yourself working in Alaska tomorrow."

Brady stepped back, but he was ready to make good on his threat. Melanie might have a few secrets, but Brady was sure he knew the real woman inside. And she was no terrorist.

"Now I'm willing to put your involvement with Ms. Parsons to good use. If you can get us some evidence of wrong doing…perhaps we can work out a deal."

"Sir, I am stating again for the record that I believe in her innocence to any involvement in this crime. In addition, I was planning to tell you I have an idea for catching the thieves in the act."

"An idea, huh?" The captain patted his chin thoughtfully for a moment. Tapping his earpiece, the captain spoke Randall Miko's name and connected to Randall's earpiece. "Miko, get your ass in here now."

A minute later there was a knock on the door and Randall popped his head inside.

"Yes, sir?"

"When I say get your ass in here I mean in my office, not hanging outside my door."

Randall flushed in annoyance and quickly entered the office. Closing the door behind him, he came to attention next to his partner. Brady could sense Randall staring over at him but he kept his eyes forward, still trying to keep his temper in check.

"Torres here says he has a plan to catch the thieves. Has he shared this with you?"

"Uh, no sir, not yet." Randall sounded surprised and a bit hurt, as if he'd been deliberately left out of the loop.

"Well Torres, why don't the two of you sit down and you can let us both in on your little plot."

Sitting down, Brady said. "I have a friend who has an article from the time period from when the burglaries are occurring. We use this article as bait for the thieves and stake out the warehouse. Agent Miko recently discovered they are using a low level EM pulse to disrupt the security vids, so we would have to have someone on site." Randall threw Brady a grateful look at being recognized for his work.

"Miko, when did you find out about this EM pulse?" The captain was looking at Randall thoughtfully.

"Just this morning, sir. In fact, Agent Torres pointed out this calls into question the validity of the Purist angle sir. They most likely wouldn't be using EM technology since they don't like technology of any kind." Randall returned the kudos favor, letting Brady know he had been listening earlier.

"What is this *article* you have access to?"

Brady had taken a holopic of the wedding dress before he left Melanie's house this morning. Tapping his earpiece he brought up the picture.

"It's a wedding dress from 1878."

"That's a wedding dress? It's not even white." Randall was staring at the plum colored dress in bemusement.

"I know. I was just as surprised as you. But I've been told the wedding dresses of this era were rarely white."

"It looks hot and uncomfortable."

Although he kept silent, Brady agreed with Randall. The dress had a high neck, long sleeves and swept the floor. It had the thick look of a clothing item made with natural fibers, rather than the cool synthetics of today.

As uncomfortable as it looked, Brady could just imagine Melanie in the dress, her waist cinched tight to emphasize the bustle on her ass. Just thinking about getting her out the dress was making him hot. Teasing and tempting her as he unbuttoned each and every button until he had her lying exposed before him. It certainly made him realize why men of that era covered up their women.

"We aren't looking at the damn thing as fashion experts. I want to know if it's going to work as bait." The captain's comments immediately broke through Brady's daydream.

"I can get the dress today and take it to the warehouse. We can put out the word a new item is being added to the collection and then set up the sting operation."

The captain sat silently for a moment, his head bent in thought, obviously contemplating Brady's plan. Finally he looked up and addressed Randall. "Send me the information on the security vids. I think we need to follow up on this EM pulse question. If this really does eliminate the Purists, we need to have some answers. Torres, stay for a minute so I can discuss one other thing with you."

Randall nodded and quickly exited the office. Brady knew he'd be bombarded with questions as soon as he left the captain's office. Randall was an old-fashioned gossip and wouldn't let him get away with 'no comment' regarding what happened. Brady was going to have to decide if he was ready to trust his new partner or not.

"I assume your friend with the dress is the Parsons woman?"

"Yes sir."

"Hmm, this plan of yours better work, Torres, or you might be back to writing air traffic tickets for DCPD."

Chapter Five

Melanie walked into work as if she were walking on air, floating above all the flotsam and jetsam of the harsh realities of life. Brady's total domination of her body last night was a dream come true. Only two weeks into their relationship, Melanie had thought Brady was the ideal man, interesting to talk to and sexy as sin, but as usual she had been worried about that final component. Last night had erased all her worries.

"Melanie, did you hear we were on the news downloads this morning?" Harold's eyes shone behind his glasses—intent on ruining her good mood, no doubt.

"No, something good I hope?"

"It was about the burglaries and how we were getting new donations to the collection to offset the missing items. I don't know anything about new items, Melanie, do you?"

Melanie had a sick feeling in her stomach that she knew exactly what the new item might be—her wedding dress. Her sick feeling turned to dread as she spotted Stan coming into the cataloguing room. She could tell there was going to be trouble by the look of malice on his face.

"Melanie, I want to speak with you right now."

Stan strode toward her double time. Not wanting another public confrontation like yesterday, Melanie decided to send Harold out of the line of fire before Stan reached them.

"Harold, why don't you start working and I'll join you as soon as Mr. Johnson and I finish our discussion?"

Harold looked at Stan bearing down on them and Melanie could tell he was scared to death. But he suddenly straightened up to his five-foot-six-and-a-half feet, prepared to stand his ground.

"I'll support you Melanie. You won't have to face him alone." She could swear she almost saw tears glistening in his eyes. Fortunately for him, she'd rather speak frankly with Stan, something she really couldn't afford to do with witnesses around.

"No Harold, that's okay. Stan and I need privacy to discuss a few issues. Go ahead and get started and I'll join you in a few minutes. Thanks." Melanie shooed him away as Stan finally reached her.

"We need to talk." Melanie could tell she shocked him by speaking first—most likely with the very words he'd anticipated using. Stan only liked confrontational situations if he was the one doing the confronting. She intended to turn the tables on him.

"Why don't we go into my office?" Not waiting for a reply, Melanie headed into her office and took a seat behind her desk. Unbeknownst to Stan, she quickly hit the holo-vid recorder she had in her office. She wanted to ensure there was a record of this particular conversation if she ever needed it.

Stan followed her into the office and, surprisingly, closed the door. Leaning back against it, he eyed her until she felt as if she were a bug under a digital scope.

"I don't know what you think you're doing, but you won't get away with it."

Stan's off-the-wall remark had her puzzled. "I really have no idea to what you are referring."

"Listen to Miss High and Mighty speaking. Your family won't be able to protect you forever you know." Stan began pacing around the small room, driving Melanie batty.

"Stan, why don't we keep your personal feelings out of this and get to the point."

Stan flopped into the chair, leaning forward to sneer at her. "I got the news downloads about a new acquisition. Since all new donations come through my office I figured it had to be you trying to pull a fast one."

"Please enlighten me how the Smithsonian getting a new acquisition equates to me pulling a fast one."

"Your family must be protecting you. If they donate something the news won't be about the burglaries, it'll be about the donation. They're trying to save your ass. But I'm going to make sure the news crews stay on the real story—we have a curator who can't stop losing things. How do you think that will look?" Stan had the look of someone who just pulled off a major coup.

"I think it'll look like my boss is a moron." Melanie had to suppress the laughter bubbling up at the twin looks of shock and horror on his face.

"You're always trying to make me look bad."

"I think you do a fine job of that all on your own." Melanie was sick and tired of getting blamed for his inability to lead. "If you hadn't cut the security budget last year there would have been guards as well as surveillance equipment and maybe someone would have thought twice about robbing the nation's museum. Instead it's become a free for all."

Stan stood up abruptly, knocking the chair over in the process. His earlier bravado gone, he now looked just livid and witless.

"Listen to me. I'll smear your name not only in this town but in every professional organization in the country. You're a Traditionalist, and everyone knows they're the ones who are behind these thefts. That's why the UAS was investigating. So you better watch your step or you might find yourself not only looking for another job, but trying to fight your way out of a prison sentence."

Melanie rose, coming around the desk and facing him toe to toe. "You know damn well I had nothing to do with these burglaries and your petty little need for vengeance is the only reason you've decided to put me in the line of fire. I refuse to allow you to threaten and accuse me in my own office. Get out, now!"

"You can act all brave if you want to, it won't change the facts."

"Exactly, and I've got truth on my side." Melanie turned and sat back down at her desk, a smile of satisfaction on her face.

"Dream on." Stan's lame comeback almost had her in stitches. He really was a pathetic man. "Besides, I came here about the acquisition. What do you know about it?"

Melanie silently considered what to say. She didn't really want to tell him about the scheme Brady had mentioned to her last night. For one thing, she didn't want to reveal her relationship to the dress, let alone her relationship to Brady and the UAS. She figured the UAS had agreed to his plan and leaked it to the news media sources. But they hadn't discussed who would know about the scheme itself. Better to be safe than sorry. Melanie decided to stick with the truth as much as possible without revealing anything personal.

"I know the item is a dress and it's an anonymous donation. I haven't received it yet so there is no further information at this time."

Stan narrowed his eyes, staring at her as if he could pop off the top of her head and look inside to get the answers he wanted. Melanie remained silent, knowing if she added anything else it would just look suspicious. Stan finally gave up and turned on his heel, grasping the handle and swinging the door open.

"You better watch your back." He spat in a final parting shot. Walking through the door he slammed it, rattling the items in her office.

"Same to you, buddy," Melanie muttered as she ended the holo-vid recording. Just as she rose to join Harold, her earpiece buzzed, indicating an incoming message and she sank back into her chair. *Some days it just doesn't pay to get out of bed.*

"Hello, Melanie Parsons speaking."

"You've got the sexiest voice." Brady's own sultry voice caressed her ear.

Melanie's insides suddenly felt molten. He could make her hot just with the sound of his voice.

"Thanks. You're not so bad yourself."

"No comparison, baby. I need you to do me a favor." Brady suddenly was all business and Melanie sat up, intrigued.

"Okay, what do you need?"

Brady groaned and chuckled. "Don't tempt me. It's about the dress."

"Oh, well before you ask for your favor, I've got to tell you something. My boss was asking questions about the dress and since I wasn't sure who you wanted to know about it, I kind of hedged the truth a bit."

"Good girl. The captain doesn't want too many people involved in this for fear of a leak. Anyway, I need you to go get the dress during your lunch hour so it's in your workroom by five o'clock tonight."

"Okay, but why?"

"We're going to start the sting tonight. That's why all the news media is buzzing about the new acquisition. I'm first on stake-out tonight so I'll be coming by to set up as soon as everyone has gone home."

Melanie's disappointment was boundless. She'd been hoping they could get together tonight and talk about where their relationship was heading. She felt like she was living on pins and needles in the uncertainty. She'd even planned to dress extra special in hopes that they'd be getting together.

"You still there?"

"Yes, sorry. Is there anything else?"

"Can you stick around after everyone goes home to let me in and help me set up?"

"Of course." Great, now she was a handyman's helper.

"I wish we could have more time together, but as soon as this case is solved maybe we can both take time off and get away."

"I'd like that." Melanie felt warmed by his words, hopeful in the thoughts of their future.

"Good. I'll see you tonight then."

"Bye." Melanie sat there for a moment, listening to the dial tone as Brady broke the connection between them. Finally shaking herself out of her stupor, she clicked the receiver off and headed out to begin work with Harold.

CR80

Hustling Harold out the door at five o'clock had been a delicate balancing act. The man was totally dedicated and when she mentioned she might stay late to work on some things he practically fell all over himself to offer to stay and help her. Melanie finally had to pretend to leave. She circled around the building and came back in after she saw him get on the metro.

Walking back into the office, Melanie was startled when a hand reached out and grabbed her arm. Turning swiftly to fight off her attacker, she subsided as soon as she recognized Brady in the darkness. Smacking him in the shoulder, she pulled away.

"You scared the life out of me. How did you get in here?"

"We're working with the head of Smithsonian security and I came down with him from the main office."

"Lights on, usual setting." Melanie ordered and a calming glow filled the room.

"Where were you?" Brady's tone held a hint of something, but Melanie wasn't sure what. Almost a combination of concern and displeasure.

"I'm not good at the cloak and dagger stuff. When I tried to get Harold out of here he wanted to stay to help."

"The man is in love with you."

Melanie stared at Brady in astonishment. Then she started to laugh. "No, he's not. He's my assistant. We're just coworkers."

"Take it from me, Harold is in love with you."

Melanie rolled her eyes. "You barely know him. You only met him for what, five minutes the other day? How would you know he's in love with me?"

"First, I have hours of holo-vids of the two of you working together. Second, a man knows these things. Third, I don't want to talk about Harold, I want to talk about you."

"Me, what about me?" Melanie felt like she was in a whirlwind, with Brady changing directions so fast it made her head spin.

"When were you going to tell me that you're from a Traditionalist family?"

Melanie stood frozen in place. She'd never mentioned the specifics about her family because it had always colored every relationship she'd ever been in. Either the guys were excited to be dating a woman from a rich Traditionalist family or they were disgusted by her family's Traditionalist values. When she'd moved to Washington D.C. she'd decided to keep her family in Philadelphia and out her love life.

"Why, does it matter to you?" Melanie waited in anticipation of his answer, hoping against hope he'd say no.

"I don't care who your family is or how much money they have. I care about the fact you felt the need to hide something from me. Do we have a trust issue?"

"No, we don't have a trust issue. It never mattered to me. I'm sorry I didn't tell you." Melanie shivered as she stared into Brady's eyes, although she wasn't frightened of him.

"I accept your apology, but I think a punishment is in order."

Melanie started at his words. "Hey now, I told you I was sorry."

"I decide when and why you get punishments, not you. Besides, you like what I do to you."

Melanie couldn't deny his words. As soon as he mentioned punishment she could feel her cream begin to flow. He didn't even need to touch her and she was getting turned on.

Pushing her up against the desk, Brady began to pull her skirt up her legs, trailing his fingers along her thighs. He groaned in appreciation when he realized she had on thigh-high stockings. As he moved his hands up further, she could tell by the flare of desire in his eyes when he discovered she was not wearing panties or a thong, but a tiny little G-string that barely covered anything at all.

"Were you expecting someone to discover this hidden package?"

"Expecting, no. Hoping, yes. Do you like it?"

"Hell yes, I like it. I think we need to do some exploring of our own tonight."

Chapter Six

Intent on Melanie, Brady barely heard the noise coming from the other room. But the words that soon followed broke through his haze like a splash of cold water.

"Agent Torres, are you in here?"

Breaking away from Melanie, Brady struggled to regain his control. He couldn't let himself forget he was here for a job. Unfortunately, when he was alone with Melanie good sense usually went out the window.

"In here." Brady called out, directing security toward the office.

"Ah, there you are. Ms. Parsons. I didn't see you leave. I wondered if you were still here."

"Hi, John. I was just getting the dress ready." Brady watched as Melanie pulled the dress out the carrying bag.

"Hard to believe someone would want to break in here just to get to a dress." John reached forward as if he was going to touch the material of the dress, but Melanie pulled it away from his grasp.

"It's very delicate. I'm still not sure if I should leave it here." Melanie bit her bottom lip, worry creasing her brow. Although Brady didn't like to see her worried, it annoyed him a bit that she was still concerned about his ability to protect her family heirloom.

"Everything will be fine. Now where would you usually put a new acquisition?"

"Out here." Melanie left the office and headed into the large cataloguing room, closely followed by Brady and John. Brady watched appreciatively as her hips swayed while she walked, gently rolling with every step.

Unfortunately, he wasn't the only one enjoying the view. He stared hard at John, cautioning him away from Melanie with just one look. John smiled in response, apparently reading the warning.

Melanie stopped in front of an open containment pod and gently placed the dress inside. As she closed the lid, Brady noted she programmed some information into the keypad and the pod sealed, preserving the integrity of dress.

"This will keep the dress safe from any harm from the environment."

"Okay, now it's our turn." Brady turned to John. Squatting down, they began pulling out wires from the bag John carried.

"What's all this?" Melanie peered over his shoulder. He could smell the sweet fruity scent of her perfume and Brady had to concentrate on answering her question. It didn't help when he noticed John's smirking face. The man was just asking to be punched.

"Since the thieves have been disabling the security's technology, we decided to try some old fashioned methods. These are trip wires. We'll set them up close to the ground and when they are triggered it will send out an alarm. The doors to this room will automatically close, sealing anyone inside."

"Hmm, how long will it take to set up?"

"It may take us a while. You can go ahead and head home since we have the dress taken care of."

"No, I've got some work in my office. If you don't mind I'll stick around until you're done so we can talk."

Brady nodded and watched as Melanie walked back to her office.

"So, you were able to defrost the ice queen." At John's unexpected question Brady turned back towards him.

"What's that supposed to mean?"

John held up his hands in surrender, chuckling as he spoke. "Don't take it the wrong way, man. I'm happy for her. Just surprised. I think every man in this building has asked her out at one time or another and most, if not all, have been turned down flat. And those she did agree to see never got a second date."

"What makes you think I've had a second date?"

John laughed aloud. "Come on, I'm not blind. There's a hell of a lot more than just a second date between you two. I'm not sure what I interrupted earlier, but I'd say it's a good thing the security vids for Ms. Parsons's office are disabled."

Brady was surprised at this information, wondering if there was any link to the burglaries. "Why are they disabled?"

"Ms. Parsons asked for them to be removed, but we couldn't do that so we disabled them instead. She said it was because it made her feel creepy to be watched. But I think it also had something to do with her boss. He used to 'review' the vids on a regular basis before she got them turned off."

Brady finished setting up the wires as he contemplated this new information. Although he couldn't see how it related to the burglaries at all, it still bothered him. He finally realized it was because he didn't like the idea of Melanie's boss scrutinizing her. Not only was it creepy, to borrow her phrase, Brady was jealous of any man who observed her in an unguarded moment. He didn't enjoy the fact other men were watching what he considered to be strictly his.

"So were you one of those men who asked her out?"

"No sir. If I were twenty years younger and didn't have a wife at home, I'd have been waiting in line like everyone else. Of course, I still like to watch." John guffawed at Brady's expression.

They finished the rest of the work in silence, setting up the trip wires around the dress and access points to the room.

"Thanks for your help." Brady shook John's hand in appreciation for not only his assistance with the set up, but for his earlier words as well.

"No problem. I hope you catch the bastards. They're making us all look bad." John made his way out the room, closing the door behind him.

Brady headed back toward the office and Melanie. It was time to finish what he'd started earlier. Walking into the office, Brady stopped for a moment and stared at Melanie. She had gotten comfortable, kicking off her shoes and at some point while waiting for him, she had lowered the lights and decided to lay her head down for a moment. Her hair was spread out like a halo where she had fallen asleep at her desk with her head cushioned on her arms.

Walking over to her, Brady smoothed her hair away from her face and watched as she blinked her eyes, slowly waking up. Upon seeing him standing there, Melanie smiled up at him, causing his heart to clench in his chest. He'd never thought he was ready to settle down, but watching Melanie greet him with a smile every morning upon waking was something he hadn't known he craved until just now.

"Hey baby, you should have gone home."

Melanie sat up slowly and stretched, pulling the fabric of her blouse tightly against her breasts. At some point she must have decided to take off her bra because her breasts were clearly visible under the sheer material. Brady's cock perked up in interest at the sight.

"No, I wanted to wait for you. I wanted to find out what my punishment was going to be."

Listening to Melanie refer to her punishment in such a matter of fact way made Brady's cock more than perk up—it came to attention.

"Are you looking forward to your punishment?"

Melanie paused for a moment before answering. "I don't know. If I say 'yes' am I depraved?"

Brady pulled her up from her chair and into his arms. "No baby, you're not depraved. You control almost every aspect of your life. In this one area you are ready for someone else to be in control. That's not depravity, it is intelligence. Don't let the dictates of society tell you how you are supposed to act."

Melanie laughed softly. "You're so good for my ego. I do enjoy what we've done together and I want more."

Brady lifted Melanie and sat her on the desk, pushing her skirt up until it was around her hips and then pulling her legs apart and stepping between them.

"So you want more, huh? Is that why you took off your bra?"

"I hate wearing that thing. You'd think after a couple hundred years they could come up with a better garment to hold up a woman's breasts, but no."

"I like seeing you without the bra, your breasts straining the buttons of this poor blouse."

Brady pushed against a button, forcing it to slip free. The slopes of her breasts were on display for his gaze. Melanie squirmed as he watched her. Brady decided this would be the perfect opportunity to fulfill one of his fantasies.

"I want to see you touch yourself." Stepping back, Brady sat in the chair she just vacated, relaxing as it conformed to his body. "Unbutton your blouse."

Melanie quickly freed the rest of her buttons, allowing the blouse to fall open, exposing her breasts to his gaze.

"What should I do?"

"How do you like to touch yourself? Show me."

Melanie licked her lips, eliciting an accompanying groan from Brady. He didn't know why he was torturing himself, but watching her pleasure herself was too good to pass up. Cupping her breasts, Melanie gently kneaded the flesh before grazing each nipple with a thumb, teasing the hardened nubs. She moaned at the contact and then grasped each nipple between a thumb and finger, rolling back and forth before gently scraping the tips with her nails.

"More, show me more."

It was as if Melanie could read his mind, although it probably wasn't too difficult to figure out where his mind was. She scooted to the edge of the desk and slipped her hand inside the tiny G-string, rubbing herself back and forth, her head falling back as her strokes became firmer. Unfortunately the material and her hand obstructed Brady's view. He could hold out no longer and pushed himself forward, between her legs.

"Lay back." He ordered harshly. "I've got to taste you."

Melanie complied immediately, lying back on her elbows so she could still see down the length of her body. He loved that she wanted to watch him licking her pussy. Taking her G-string, he ripped it from her body, too rushed to be gentle.

The aroma of her arousal hit him and he salivated at the thought of tasting her spicy cream. Trailing a finger up her thigh, Brady watched as she shivered in reaction to his touch. Moving his finger higher, he traced the crease of her pussy, gathering the juices collected there. Bringing his finger to his lips, he licked it clean, but the brief taste of her only left him hungry for more.

Brady lowered his head and ran his tongue along her slit, coming close to her clit, but not quite touching it. Melanie moaned and arched her hips toward him. Gently parting her folds, Brady explored the inner recesses of her pussy, before moving to her clit and nibbling at it.

"Yes, God, Brady, more, more." Melanie was no longer propped on her elbows, but flat on her back, her feet pressed against his shoulders as she pressed her pussy into his mouth. Sucking her clit into his mouth, Brady let her ride out her orgasm before finally releasing her clit and letting her legs fall.

Standing up, Brady quickly divested himself of his clothing until he was standing naked before her. Finally recovered from her orgasm, Melanie stared up at him, her desire banked slightly but in no way fully satisfied.

"I was going to withhold your orgasm as your punishment, but you looked so beautiful coming on my tongue I couldn't help myself."

Melanie smiled at him in thanks, but then a frown creased her brow.

"What is it?"

"I wanted you to come inside me, but I don't have any inhalers here." The birth control and disease protection devices they had taken last night only lasted twenty four hours and it was too close to that time to be sure the protection would still be viable.

"Good thing I was thinking ahead." Brady smiled, holding up the two inhalers he had pulled out his pocket earlier.

"Expecting to get laid tonight?" Melanie grabbed one of the inhalers from him and took a quick puff as he did the same with his own.

"Expecting, no. Hoping, yes," Brady parroted her earlier words.

Leaning down, Brady captured her lips in a kiss, exploring her mouth before moving down her neck to tease the soft skin there. Reaching down between them, Brady stroked her pussy, rubbing the pad of his thumb over her sensitive clit. Melanie bucked against his massaging digit, her nail digging deep into his shoulders.

"Come inside me now, Brady. I want you to fill me up."

Never one to disappoint a lady, Brady grasped his cock and centered it at her heated core. Pressing forward he penetrated her slowly, inching his way inside as Melanie gasped and clawed at him, urging him to move faster.

"Easy baby, we've got all night."

Melanie whimpered with her need, begging him. "Please Brady, don't tease me. I want hard and fast."

Brady knew he was torturing himself just as much as her, his need for her so great he was barely holding the reins of his control. He wanted her to experience the pleasure of delayed gratification, knowing that she relied on him to gain her pleasure.

Finally seated deep inside, Brady began to move, thrusting slowly at first, but rapidly gaining speed. Brady could feel the tightening in his balls and desperately began pounding into Melanie. Reaching between them, he thumbed her clit and her body arched in reaction, practically coming off the desk. Her pussy clamped tightly against his cock for one maddening minute and then a million flutters surrounded him as she came. He gave one final thrust and released his seed inside her.

Collapsing on her prostrate body, Brady struggled to regain his breath. He could feel Melanie cushioning his body, her hands gently stroking his back. The contentment he felt right now was something he wanted to have forever. Unfortunately, this was not the evening for the long term relationship discussion he wanted to have. But soon, they would be talking about their future.

Chapter Seven

Although she'd been up half the night, Melanie walked into work with a spring in her step. All her previous doubts about Brady and their relationship had melted away and she could finally feel free to be who she really was. It was a heady sensation.

"Good morning Harold, how are you?"

Her assistant looked up from the table he'd been working at and smiled sadly at her. His usual fawning enthusiasm was missing this morning. "Good morning, Melanie."

"Harold, what's wrong? You look down today."

"Oh, nothing. Just not feeling too well."

"I hope you're not getting sick. Maybe you should have stayed home." Melanie was as dedicated as could be, but she would never come to work sick and wished everyone would do the same.

"No, no, I'm not sick." Harold bent back toward his work, giving no further explanation.

Melanie shrugged and headed toward her office. She was in too good a mood to allow Harold's bad one to ruin her day. Melanie stared at her desk, wondering how it could look so innocuous in the daylight when last night it had been so much more.

"Did you come back to work last night?" Harold's question startled Melanie from her daydream. Glancing up she saw him standing in her doorway.

"Ah, yes, I did. How did you know?"

"I saw the dress."

"Yes, it's beautiful isn't it?" Melanie smiled at Harold, but her mind was whirling. After making love last night, Brady had eventually sent her home and stayed the rest of the night for the stakeout. Early this morning he had contacted her before she left for work, to tell her he'd removed all the evidence of the trip wires and was heading home to get some sleep. She hoped he hadn't forgotten something—which might have clued Harold into the set up.

"It's from the late nineteenth century, correct?"

"Yes, a wedding dress from that time period."

Harold nodded, rubbing his hands together. "Yes, I thought so. A perfect Traditionalist item."

"I guess you could say so." Melanie thought Harold's comment was a bit odd, but of course, so was he.

"Well, I better get back to work. Sorry to bother you."

"No bother, Harold. I'll be right out as soon as I check my messages."

Harold left the office and Melanie began scrolling through her messages. After a few minutes though, she began to think back to last night again and Brady. She wondered what the future held for them. Always eschewing her family's Traditionalist values, she was shocked to realize she was thinking about long term commitment and—she could barely even think it—marriage.

"You slut." For the second time today Melanie was startled from her thoughts by someone standing at her office door. Stan's face was red and blotchy and he stood before her practically shaking.

"What did you just call me?" Melanie stood to confront him, her hand ready to contact security at a moment's notice.

"You heard me. I saw you, last night. Here with the UAS Agent. Fucking him on this desk." Stan hit the desk with the palm of his hand, causing Melanie to jump back.

"You were spying on me?" Melanie felt sick, disgusted this pervert had watched them. "Wait a minute, I know you were out of town last night. How did you see…?"

Stan snarled at her. "You always thought you were so smart. When you had those security recorders disabled, I installed my own devices. I knew I'd have to watch you and see, I was right. You're trying to take my job."

"You are a sick, depraved man. I don't know why you think I want your job, but I don't. I just want to be left alone to do my own job, thank you very much."

"Then why are you working with the UAS, planning secret operations without my approval? I've got to say though, I was surprised by the show I saw here last night. I didn't think Traditionalists were so…kinky."

"You disgust me. Who's the kinky one, you pervert? Those holo-vid recordings are a violation of my civil rights. I want them returned and the recording devices removed. Do you understand me? If they aren't, I'm going to bring you up on charges and smear you in the media."

"Please, I'm sure you don't want those recordings to fall into the wrong hands. Your pretty face, and other pretty parts, all over the news media would certainly embarrass your family."

Melanie's face burned at the thought of her love life on display. Not only would it embarrass her family, it most likely would cause Brady to lose his job. On the other hand, she wasn't some flighty female who was going to let this piece of trash walk all over her.

"You've heard my terms, now I'm leaving for the day. You can take the time to remove the recording devices and I expect to have those holo-vids tomorrow." Melanie picked up her purse and grabbed her coat, hoping she wasn't making the worst mistake of her life. *How could this morning, when things were looking so good, turn to crap so fast?*

Stan's face was a comical combination of maliciousness and confusion. He obviously still believed he had the upper hand, but couldn't quite figure out why Melanie wasn't falling into line. *God save me from stupid people.*

"Oh, I'll see you tomorrow all right. On the news media vids with your legs spread wide." Stan turned and exited her office and Melanie sank into her chair, her coat and purse still in hand. She realized she was shaking, probably aftereffects from the shock of the encounter.

"Melanie, is everything okay?" Harold stood in the doorway, his eyes full of concern.

"Yes Harold, thanks." Harold turned to leave, but Melanie called him back. "Harold, I'm going to send a few communications and then I'm heading home for the day. If any emergencies come up you can contact me at home."

Harold looked as if he were going to say more, but then just nodded his head and left the office. Melanie sighed heavily before tapping her ear piece and beginning her contacts.

CR80

Melanie sat working at the desk in her home office, trying to concentrate on the figures swimming in front of the computer screen. Pushing herself back, she decided to take a break. The budgets were probably all going to have to be double-checked since she doubted she even had ten percent of her thoughts on work today.

Before making good on her promise to leave for the day, Melanie had contacted her parents and sister. Forced to leave messages, she only told her parents she was being blackmailed by her boss and needed to talk to them. Worried about how they would take another scandal in the family in less than a year, Melanie decided to leave a lot more detail in her message to her sister, hoping she had some ideas about how they could cushion the blow to their family's reputation.

Her older sister Melissa had divorced last year, the first Parsons in a three hundred year history. Traditionalist families didn't believe in divorce. In fact, because they usually had the more rigorous commitment wedding instead of just the promise ceremony, they were required by law to attempt counseling for a period of time before divorce.

Their parents had been able to get a waiver to the law after Melissa's husband beat her so severely she lost the child she was carrying. It was one of the reasons Melanie couldn't understand why her family continued to cling to the Traditionalist values. Sure, her parent's marriage had turned out fine, but as Melissa could attest, a nightmare might be just around the corner.

Thinking about marriage made her think about Brady. She had tried to contact him as well, but he must have turned off all incoming communications when he went home to sleep. Her message only said she needed to talk to him about last night. She was dreading the time when he got the communication and contacted her, worried about his reaction. He could very well lose his job because of this fiasco.

The doorbell chiming sent Melanie flying down the stairs. Not expecting anyone, especially during the day, she figured Brady must have woken up early and gotten her message. Wiping her hands on her pants, she couldn't believe how nervous she was. That was probably why she didn't check to see who was at the door.

"Melanie, darling, are you okay?" Melanie's parents and sister stood in her doorway, waiting to be invited inside.

"Oh my God, I can't believe you're all here." Melanie quickly moved from the doorway to let them in.

"We couldn't let you face this alone." Douglas Parsons briefly kissed her cheek before enveloping her in a giant bear hug.

She thought she had been doing well holding things together, but the love and warmth surrounding her caught her emotions off guard and she began to cry.

"Hey now pumpkin, what's all this?" Her dad wiped her tears away and they sat together on the couch, with her mother on the other side.

"Why don't I go fix drinks for everyone?" Melissa went into the kitchen while Melanie did her best to get her emotions under control.

"Thank you so much for your love and support. I still can't believe you came here."

"Oh sweetheart, it's not a long trip. Besides, I want your father to kick your boss's ass."

Melanie burst into laughter. Miranda Parsons never, ever swore and to hear the word "ass" come out her mouth seemed to break Melanie's bad mood.

"What's all this frivolity in here? I thought we were going to be mopey and depressed." Melissa came into the room with a tray of drinks for everyone. Melanie jumped up to help, giving her sister a brief hug.

"Why don't Melissa and I rustle up something to eat?" Melanie pulled her sister into the kitchen, intent on giving her the third degree.

"You only enlisted me to help because you hate to cook," Melissa complained with a laugh.

"No, I wanted to talk to you. We haven't kept in touch like I wanted and for you to come down here with Mom and Dad, well…I'm touched."

"Touched in the brain it sounds like, screwing your *boyfriend* on the desk in your office."

Melanie slugged her sister in the arm before pulling food out of the cupboard. "Ha, ha. It's not as sordid as it sounds, although it looks pretty damaging on the vids."

"I'll bet. How detailed did you get with Mom and Dad, by the way?"

"No detail at all. I just told them I was being blackmailed. I figured you could comfort Mom and Dad in Philadelphia, not encourage them to come here."

"Encourage them? You've got it all wrong. I've been holding them back all day. By the way, Dad's already run a background check on your *boyfriend*."

"Will you stop saying 'boyfriend'? We aren't teenagers any more. His name is Brady. And how did Dad find out about him?"

"I accidentally let it slip. Anyway, Dad almost flipped when he found out Brady wasn't a Traditionalist. Although being an agent for the UAS has given him a slight benefit in the ratings."

"It's not like we're getting married or anything, so I don't know why they care if he's a Traditionalist or not."

"Well, be prepared. Mom and Dad both hate what happened to me and they don't plan to see history repeat itself. They are going to rake any guy you bring to them over the coals."

"Why do you think I've been hiding out here?" Melanie smiled, glad she and her sister had been able to slip back into their easy banter as if there had been no break.

"Melissa, I've got to tell you something." Melanie didn't want to break the mood, but she didn't want to have any barriers between them either.

"Okay, what is it?"

"I blamed myself for what happened to you. I never liked him and I kept it to myself. I always wondered—if I had spoken up, would it have made a difference?"

Melissa grabbed Melanie, hugging her tight. "Is this why you left town so suddenly after I got out of the hospital?"

Melanie nodded. "I couldn't face you. I felt terrible. I just wanted to live on my own for a while and get away from all the Traditionalist values I thought I hated so much because he'd hurt you so badly."

"Listen to me. First, this wasn't your fault. I probably would have married him anyway, because I was young and stupid. Second, this has nothing to do with Traditionalist values. He was an asshole, plain and simple. I just thank God he's out of my life."

"I love you, sis."

"I love you too."

Melanie and Melissa hugged, but were broken apart by the doorbell chiming again, signaling another arrival. Melanie ran to the door, knowing this time it couldn't be anyone but Brady. As she opened the door, he stood there, looking anxious.

"Baby, what's going on? I got your message and you sounded upset." He peered into her face and reached up to swipe a tear she must have missed earlier. "Why have you been crying?"

Melanie wrapped her arms around him, grateful for his concern. She just hoped he didn't hate her when he heard the whole story.

"Melanie, who's at the door?"

"It's Brady. We'll be right there."

Brady raised his eyebrows, obviously wondering what was going on.

"My parents and sister showed up after I contacted them this morning," she explained in a whisper as she stepped back to let him into the house.

"Okay. Why are we whispering?" Brady closed the door behind him, slipping his arm around her shoulders as they headed down into the living room.

"Because young man, she's giving you the heads-up you're going to be grilled."

Chapter Eight

"Daddy!" Brady chuckled at Melanie's outraged shriek. He wasn't scared of Melanie's father.

"You can start the flamer at any time, sir, but can we hold off on the grilling until I hear more about what's going on?"

"You mean, she didn't tell you?" Another woman, close to Melanie's age, was barely controlling her laughter. *This must be Melissa.*

"Melissa, this is no laughing matter, young lady." Their mother's words caused both girls to roll their eyes. She turned back to Brady, a smile on her face. "Ignore these two hooligans. I'm Miranda Parsons and you must be Brady Torres."

Shaking her hand as Melanie began to apologize profusely, Brady could see the love surrounding her family. He only hoped Melanie was willing to let him in.

"Brady, this is my father, Douglas Parsons."

As he shook her father's hand he asked, "Do all the female members of your family have names starting with an M?"

"It's a silly tradition…" Melanie began to explain.

"Melanie, no tradition is silly. It may be odd, but we've enjoyed it over the years. I often tease Douglas he married me because of my name."

"Well now, introductions are done. Melanie, you gave us the generalities earlier, but I think it's time we got the details." Douglas was obviously a man who liked to get down to business and quite frankly, Brady was ready to hear the entire story as well.

Melanie's face was fiery red and her sister was still trying to control her giggles. She already knew the story, Brady surmised. As they took their seats in the living room Brady was pleased when Melanie dragged him down beside her on the love seat. He noticed her parents took note of the action as well.

"Oh God, I don't know how to put this so I'm just going to come out and say it. My evil boss has a holo-vid of Brady and me making love in my office."

In the stunned silence following her words Brady kept his own immediate response to himself. He was going to kill her boss if he ever got him alone. Not only had the man violated their privacy, he'd seen Melanie naked.

Instead of letting his anger control him, Brady sat back and judged the reactions of Melanie's family. Her sister continued to look amused, but had been able to control her giggles. Her mother looked slightly shocked, but a smile hovered around her lips, as if she were pleased by at least some part of the confession. Her father looked thunderous and Brady knew if Douglas condemned Melanie, he would be in for a fight. Brady wouldn't stand by and allow anyone to say anything against her, even if it were her own father.

"Wait a minute. I thought you had the recording devices disabled." Of all the things her father might have said, this was the one thing Brady wasn't expecting. And neither was Melanie, it seemed.

"How did you know about the recorders? I told Mom about how creepy he made me feel, but I asked her not to mention it to you."

"Oh sweetheart, I can't keep secrets from your father. Besides, he needed to know."

"*Mother.*" Melanie sighed with exasperation before turning back toward her father. "He informed me today he'd put his own in after I'd had them shut down. Supposedly because he needed to watch me since I was trying to steal his job."

"Well, we've got him on civil rights violations."

Brady was pleased to see how supportive her parents were being, but unfortunately it probably wouldn't help. "True sir, but he could still have the vids sent out across the net before we could stop him."

"Sleazy bastard." Brady agreed wholeheartedly with Douglas's estimation of Stan's character.

"What does he want?" Melissa cut to the heart of the matter with her question. If they could figure out what Stan's goal was they could figure out how to outwit him.

"I don't know. He didn't really ask for anything." Melanie repeated the conversation she'd had with Stan this morning. "He's always been jealous of me and hated my position in the professional community. He even tried to blame me for the burglaries. He knows something like this will ruin my reputation. Not to mention what it'll do to the Parsons family name."

"I think both your professional reputation and the Parsons family name can hold their own. But what's this about burglaries?" Douglas asked with a frown, obviously just now hearing about them.

As Melanie explained the details of the burglaries to her family, Brady re-examined everything she had told them so far. He had a niggling feeling there was some important fact he was overlooking, but he couldn't put his finger on what it was.

"You're using the wedding dress as *bait*?" Miranda's shocked tone pulled Brady from his evaluation of the facts.

"Mom, Brady has assured me the dress is safe. Besides, we need a low tech solution to catch these thieves." Melanie's defense of him made Brady realize she not only trusted him, but she was willing to stand up to her family, taking his side.

"How is Brady keeping the dress safe if he's here with you?" Douglas' question looked as if it caught Melanie off guard for a moment, but she quickly recovered.

"I'm sure someone from the UAS is on the job." Her confidence in him was undeniable.

Brady nodded. "My partner is at the Smithsonian right now on stakeout duty. I called him before I came over and asked him to cover for me tonight. On another note though, I think you should know the UAS suspects the burglaries to be the work of Traditionalists."

"You've got to be kidding. No self-worthy Traditionalist would get involved in anything so sordid."

"Perhaps not, but the authorities aren't so sure, especially when it comes to the Purist sect. "

"Those idiots. If they could, I think they'd go back to living in the Stone Age." It was obvious Douglas had no love for the Purists.

"I don't think the Purists can be implicated in this case, simply because of the technological issues involved." Brady explained the low level EM pulse that was used to disrupt the surveillance equipment.

"Still, it's disheartening to realize the government suspects us." Miranda seemed saddened by the whole turn of the conversation.

"Most people see Traditionalists as old, rich families. They don't understand their background or value system." Melanie looked astonished by Brady's comments. Although he hadn't been raised a Traditionalist, Brady envied their tight family units and customs. It was one of the reasons he'd been pleasantly surprised by the captain's revelations of Melanie's background.

"You seem to know a lot about the subject, especially for someone who doesn't come from a Traditionalist family." Douglas was nothing if not blunt.

"You're right, I don't come from a Traditionalist family. You can't choose the family into which you were born. You can only live your life as you need to live it." Brady stared hard at Douglas, daring him to say something else. He was surprised at who spoke next however.

"Enough of all this boring conversation. We can't do anything about Melanie's boss tonight—the stakeout is covered and family values is a tedious subject. So let's get to the good stuff. How long have you two been going out?" Melissa's eyes twinkled at Melanie's shocked expression, but Brady was interested in her answers.

"My personal life is just that, personal."

"Not really, sis, if your boss makes good on his threat and tells the world about your rendezvous." Melissa wasn't letting Melanie escape so easily.

"Fine, we've been dating for two months."

"And you're obviously sleeping together, so the relationship must be serious."

"Melissa!" Melanie's eyes darted back and forth between her parents, who, surprisingly, were sitting silently watching the discussion between the sisters unfold, and Brady, who was very interested in hearing Melanie's answer.

"What? I'm pretty sure it's the question of the hour."

"Okay, enough." Douglas finally interceded, much to Brady's annoyance. "Let's leave these two to talk and we'll go check into our hotel."

Melissa looked irritated to be denied her answers, but eventually Melanie's family said their goodbyes and Brady and Melanie were finally alone.

"So are you mad at me?"

Melanie's question surprised Brady. "Why should I be mad at you?"

"Oh, I don't know. I may get you fired from your job because a vid of us having sex in my office could hit the net at any time. Or maybe because my bratty older sister is practically insinuating we should be walking down the aisle since we've done the deed."

Brady chuckled as he pulled Melanie into his arms. "I think I can handle it if my bare ass makes it onto the net, although having the rest of the world see you naked may put me over the edge. As for your sister, I was kind of hoping to hear your answer to her questions."

Melanie stared up at him, surprise and doubt flitting across her face. "I never thought I'd want to get married, be committed and tied down. I never wanted to give a man so much control."

Brady concentrated on the fact she said she "never thought", rather than the rest of her words. He hoped, no prayed, he was right.

Melanie licked her lips before she continued. "But I wasn't happy. Not until I met you. And giving up control in the bedroom has made me beyond happy. I love you Brady and although I don't know what you want—I'm willing to consider marriage if you are."

Melanie shrieked as Brady picked her up and twirled her around the room. Setting her down, Brady leaned in and kissed her, putting into action his reaction to her words. "I love you too, Melanie. More than you'll ever know. I want to get married and start a family right away." Knowing her Traditionalist family though, he knew he'd have to ask her father for her hand.

Melanie stroked his face, her love shining in her eyes. "It sounds wonderful."

"So you're willing to give up control to me for the rest of your life?" Brady teased.

"Control in the bedroom, yes. I still get a say everywhere else."

"I've got no problem with your demands, but I want to make one thing clear. It's your sexual control I want, in the bedroom and everywhere else. So just remember, sex isn't limited to in the dark, behind closed doors and in bed."

Melanie blushed, but nodded. "It's not likely I'll forget. Especially if your bare ass makes it out on the net."

"I think you're begging for a spanking." Brady swatted her covered behind, but instead of shying away, Melanie pressed into him, rubbing against his growing erection.

"How about you come upstairs and give me what I need." Melanie's husky come-on had Brady ready for anything she wanted to dish out.

CB&O

Lying in bed later, Brady felt extremely satisfied. Melanie was snuggled in his arms after a bout of exceptional lovemaking. He and Melanie had declared their love for one another and he planned to talk with her parents about the wedding tomorrow. The only dark spot on his horizon was what to do about Stan Johnson and how they were going to catch the thieves.

"Son of a bitch."

Melanie woke up at his startled exclamation. "Brady, what is it?"

"I was thinking about Stan Johnson and the thieves and it suddenly occurred to me what I had been missing all night."

"You're lying in bed with me and thinking of Stan? I don't know if I like that too much."

"Very funny. I think I know how we can catch the thieves."

"Really? How?" Melanie sat up, the sheet riding down around her hips. Brady had to force himself to look away from the temptation she represented.

"If the thieves only knew about the official security recorders, there is a possibility the EM pulse wasn't directed at your office and the vids may have caught something."

"But we don't even know where they are in the office or where the feed is going. Although I suspect Stan has it directly linked to his office computer."

"I've got to contact Randall and let him know what we suspect." Brady fumbled around for his ear piece and attempted to contact Randall, but there was no response.

"Brady, you don't think the thieves have struck do you?" Melanie looked worried.

"I hope not, but I better get down there and check things out."

"I want to come with you."

"You'd better not. We don't know what we'll find."

"Forget it, Agent Torres. This isn't a bedroom issue. I'm coming." Melanie got out of bed and began to get dressed.

Brady sighed and followed her example. He figured he better get used to the fact that although he controlled Melanie in the bedroom, he'd never be completely in charge. She was too headstrong to allow it.

Chapter Nine

Walking into the artifact room at two o'clock in the morning had a completely different feeling than it did during the daylight hours. Melanie shivered in the dimly lit room and huddled behind Brady as they silently made their way through the aisles. Instead of the excited feeling of possible discovery she usually had, she instead was worried about what they might uncover.

Brady had tried again to contact his partner on their way over to the Smithsonian, but had still been unable to reach him. Melanie was also concerned about the fate of the wedding dress, although she still believed Brady would do anything in his power to ensure its protection. Unfortunately, not all things were in his power.

"Do you see any sign of Agent Miko?" Melanie whispered to Brady as he guided them around the areas where the trip wires were set up.

"Not yet."

Maneuvering around yet another trap, Melanie wondered, not for the first time, what possessed her to accompany Brady when he announced he was coming down to check things out. She wasn't an agent with the UAS. She should have left this work to those who knew what they were doing.

"Halt where you stand. I have you covered." The harshly ordered words came from out of the darkness and Melanie stopped, standing as still as a statue in a sculpture garden.

"Damn it Randall, it's me."

"Brady, what're doing here? And who's with you?"

"Hello, Agent Miko." Melanie called out, wondering where he was hiding.

"I've been trying to contact you all night. I thought something had happened." Brady sounded a bit exasperated and Melanie partially agreed with him. If they'd been able to contact him they never would have left the bed.

"My com got zapped on my way over here. I'll have to trade it in tomorrow." Randall finally made his way out of the surrounding darkness. "But what brought the two of you down here tonight?"

Melanie was suddenly glad of the dim lighting as she felt her cheeks blush with embarrassment. The first time she'd met Randall, Brady and she pretended not to know one another. It was obvious now they knew each other pretty well. Of course, if Stan got his way the entire world might know how intimately they were acquainted.

"Why don't we go to Melanie's office where we can talk?"

At Brady's suggestion the three of them trooped toward her office, continuing to avoid the trip wires set up around the room.

"It's amazing how much time and effort you guys put into setting all these things up."

"Technology is an efficient way to do business except when some newer equipment comes along to overthrow all the advances made. It's then people revert to the tried and true low-tech methods to get the job done."

Melanie was surprised by Randall's response. She had frankly considered him somewhat of a government automaton, nice enough, but a bit dim and not too polished. Instead he was proving to be an intelligent guy with obviously varied opinions. It would certainly teach her to not make such snap judgments in the future.

Reaching her office, Melanie ordered the lights on and they all sat down.

"So does someone want to tell me what's going on?"

"Melanie's boss has been secretly recording her in the office. I'm hoping the thieves don't know about the devices and they weren't affected by the EM pulse. There may be a chance we could figure out who is doing this."

"Well, let's go." Randall stood, waiting for the two of them to join him.

"We've got to figure out where the devices are hidden first and then figure out where the feed is directed."

"I might be able to help with that." The two men turned toward Melanie as she spoke. "If you find the devices I can possibly direct the feed to my computer, so it won't matter where the feed was originally going."

"I never knew you were so handy with a computer." Melanie could almost swear Brady sounded proud of her.

"Computer engineering was my major in college for a year before I changed to history. I've kept up some of my skills."

"Lucky for us." Randall looked like he was smiling at some private joke.

Brady stared hard at Randall for a moment before turning back to Melanie. "Well, it sounds like a good plan. Why don't you get started on figuring out if you can do it while we search?"

Melanie nodded and brought up the holo keyboard and screen as the two men began to empty her bookcases. Within minutes they'd found three devices. Just the reminder of Stan spying on her made her skin feel clammy. She tried to rid her mind of the thoughts of Stan possibly jerking off while watching her. Randall and Brady returned to their seats and Melanie half listened to their conversation while she began working on rerouting the computer feed for the holo-vid recorders.

"So how did you discover the secret recorders?"

Brady shifted uncomfortably in his seat, glancing briefly over at Melanie. "Melanie's boss told her when he threatened to expose her by releasing the vids on the net."

"How would watching her sitting around working on her computer all day…oooh, he got something else on the holo-vid." Randall whistled through his teeth. "The guy sounds like a sweetheart."

Melanie had glanced up as Randall realized what Stan might have seen, but she quickly lowered her head again when he winked at her. Continuing to work, she labored to track the feed through the internal network system. She figured Stan would be too lazy to install more than just the devices and had probably piggy backed onto the Smithsonian network drive.

"I found it." Melanie looked up from the computer, her face aglow with accomplishment. She quickly typed some commands into the computer and the three dimension holo-screen came up, showing the views of the three devices the men had found.

"This first one doesn't show anything except the back of her head." Randall observed as Melanie blushed fiery red.

"Why don't you bring up the next view?" Brady suggested, obviously feeling as uncomfortable as Melanie about what Stan had seen recorded from the night before.

Melanie quickly changed to the second view, which was a direct frontal observation of her sitting at the desk.

"This one is no good either. I think the last one must be the one that'll show the outer room."

"I hope so," Melanie responded as she switched to the final view.

"Damn it." Brady's exclamation expressed what they were all thinking. Although a small sliver of the door and outer room was visible, it wasn't nearly enough to get a clear picture to identify someone.

"That's too bad, Torres. It was a good idea though."

Brady opened his mouth to respond and then suddenly ordered, "Lights off."

"What…"

"Shhh, I think I heard something."

Melanie sat in the darkness, her nerves as tight as a bow string. Brady and Randall stood in the doorway, peering out into the echoing room. Unexpectedly, she thought she heard something as well. Evidently the two men had heard the same thing since they nodded to one another and then slipped from the room one at a time. Brady glanced back over his shoulder as he left, his concern for her evident in his action.

Wishing she knew what was going on, Melanie had to stop herself from squirming in her chair. Any little noise could alert the thief that someone else was there. A loud clanging pierced the silence. *The trip wire had worked.*

Melanie shivered as she heard footfalls running in the outer room. Without lights, she had no idea if Brady was the one running or if it was the thief. She soon discovered the answer as a small figure entered her office. He had no idea she was in the room until he stood at the edge of her desk.

"Melanie!"

"Harold, what are you doing here?" Melanie couldn't understand why Harold would come into work in the middle of the night. Although she was sitting here, so who was she to talk.

"I'm sorry Melanie. I'm so sorry." Harold bowed his head in defeat as it sank in to Melanie's overly tired brain—Harold was the thief they'd been searching for.

"Oh Harold, how could you?"

Harold didn't answer, but turned to leave her office. Melanie couldn't let him escape. Picking up a glass sculpture sitting on her desk she hurled it at him, hitting him the back. He went down with a crash just as Brady and Randall reached her office.

"Lights on." Melanie stood and stared at the sight before her. Randall was cuffing Harold as Brady rushed to her side.

"Are you okay?"

"I'm fine." Melanie couldn't believe how anti-climatic it felt. Although she was glad to see Harold wasn't really injured, she still couldn't believe it had been him all along.

"Why Harold?"

"I'm in love with you, Melanie." Harold's face was streaked with tears. "You never noticed me, always being more interested in your work. I thought I'd steal the items and then discover them later. You would have been so impressed with me."

"Oh Harold, I *was* impressed with your work. You should have never done something illegal just to try and make an impact on me."

"Well, it wouldn't have worked anyway, would it?" he sneered, nodding toward Brady. "You're in love with him. I thought you were better than a common whore."

"Hey now, be nice." Randall ordered, pulling back on his arms, as Brady made to lunge at Harold.

"I found your ripped panties and the inhalers. I know what you were doing in here. So I decided to steal your precious wedding dress. I was going to burn it and leave it on your desk, to discover in the morning. I wanted you to suffer like I suffered."

"Guess you weren't expecting to get caught," Brady scoffed.

"You bastard." Melanie rushed around the desk and slapped Harold, knocking his head back. "How dare you pretend to be a historian and then threaten to burn an antique? You're a fraud."

Brady pulled her back as Randall held on to Harold, barely controlling his laughter.

"She's one in a million, Torres. Or are there any more like you at home?" Randall asked quizzically.

"As a matter of fact…"

"Leave my sister out of this," Melanie groused as Randall hauled Harold away.

"So I saved your dress, keeping it safe from the evil marauder."

Melanie snorted. "The evil marauder intent on terrorism just doesn't look the same when it's Harold boo-hooing about love gone wrong."

"So, do I ever get to see you in the dress?"

"If you play your cards right. Only very special women get to wear the dress and only very special men get to see them in the dress."

"I solved the mystery, saved the dress and got to kiss the girl—I think that makes me pretty damn special."

"I didn't get a kiss. Are you kissing some other girl?"

"There are no other girls for me. And as for that kiss…" Brady took her in his arms, plundering her mouth as if delving into her soul. "I will be seeing you in that dress."

Epilogue

Six months later

The Parsons-Torres wedding was turning into the affair of the century. The entire Parsons clan was preparing to attend the wedding in the usual Traditionalist fashion. The surprise was Brady's family. Although not Traditionalists, they were not to be outdone and members of the Torres family were coming from far and wide.

Standing around watching all the guests arrive, Brady fingered the antique pocket watch Melanie had given him for a wedding gift. He wondered if she had received her gift and worried it wasn't going to seem like much compared to the expensive watch she had gifted him with. If only he could see Melanie's face, he would be able to tell if the gift was a hit.

Thinking about seeing Melanie made Brady ache. They had practically been living together for the past six months, ever since the night Harold was arrested. Brady had paid a visit to Stan the next day and had a somewhat forceful discussion with him. The sight of Harold on the news downloads walking to the courthouse in shackles may have also made an impression. Stan willingly turned over the vids to Brady with little convincing.

Stan had resigned just a few weeks later and Melanie was made director. Although the job took a lot of her time, she and Brady spent every free minute together. But ultimately, Melanie's Traditionalist upbringing kicked in and in the last week she had made Brady stay home every night, heightening the anticipation of the wedding night. Deciding to throw caution to the wind, Brady made his way through the back of the church to the area where all the women seemed to be gathered.

Although he just wanted to swing open the door, Brady forced himself to knock politely. "Melanie, are you in there?"

"Brady Torres, don't you dare come in this room!" Melanie's shriek rang out through the door.

"Why not?" Even he could hear the frustration in his voice.

"You can't see me before the wedding because it's supposed to be bad luck to see the bride in her wedding dress." Brady could hear Melanie more clearly as she obviously moved closer to the door.

"Are you in the dress?"

"Not yet."

Brady had to control his groan, his imagination running wild as to just what she might be wearing. "Well then…"

Melanie was openly laughing now. "Absolutely not. My mother would have a heart attack if I let you in here wearing only a corset."

"What's a corset?" As Melanie described the garment, Brady realized his imagination had nothing on old fashioned reality. He actually had to clinch his fist to avoid twisting the doorknob.

"I was wondering if you got my wedding gift."

"Not only did I get it, I have the sixpence in my shoe as we speak. Thank you Brady, it's perfect. Almost as perfect as you."

He had spoken with her mother and discovered the old tradition of the bride wearing something old, something new, something borrowed and something blue. Miranda told him the last sentence in the poem included a line about a sixpence in her shoe.

Although he had no idea what a sixpence was, Brady did some research and discovered it was an old form of money. Unfortunately, the coins were almost impossible to find until he discovered, just a few days before the wedding, that a local antique store had one. He'd bought the sixpence, wrapped it in a box and sent it to her home.

Forget this! Brady wasn't going a second longer without having her in his arms. "I'm coming in." Brady opened the door as screams came from inside the room. "Calm down ladies, I have my eyes closed."

Brady reached out and Melanie stepped forward into his arms. "I need to give you one last kiss as Melanie Parsons, because soon you're going to be a Torres and we'll start our own traditions. Now give me a kiss."

Melanie giggled before tugging his head down into a blazing kiss. Brady pulled her close, reacquainting himself with the feel of her soft body. He couldn't wait to see what the corset looked like on her. However, he was keeping his promise to leave her sight unseen.

Breaking the kiss, Brady ran his hand down her back and smacked her ass lightly. "Get dressed woman, there's a wedding waiting on you."

And a lifetime of happiness awaiting us.

Liz Andrews

To learn more about Liz Andrews, please visit www.lizandrews.net. Send an email to Liz Andrews at msliz@lizandrews.net.

Samhain Publishing, Ltd.

It's all about the story…

Action/Adventure
Fantasy
Historical
Horror
Mainstream
Mystery/Suspense
Non-Fiction
Paranormal
Red Hots!
Romance
Science Fiction
Western
Young Adult

http://www.samhainpublishing.com